MYSTIC
CITY

MYSTIC CITY

THEO LAWRENCE

DELACORTE PRESS

Text copyright © 2012 by The Inkhouse
Jacket art copyright © 2012 by Cliff Nielsen

All rights reserved. Published in the United States by Delacorte Press, an imprint of
Random House Children's Books, a division of Random House, Inc., New York.

Delacorte Press is a registered trademark and the
colophon is a trademark of Random House, Inc.

Visit us on the Web! randomhouse.com/teens

Educators and librarians, for a variety of teaching tools, visit us at
randomhouse.com/teachers

Library of Congress Cataloging-in-Publication Data
Lawrence, Theo.
Mystic city / Theo Lawrence. — 1st ed.
p.   cm.
Summary: In a Manhattan where the streets are under water and outcasts called
mystics have paranormal powers, Aria Rose is engaged to Thomas Foster and the
powerful Rose and Foster families—longtime enemies—are uniting politically; the
only trouble is that Aria cannot remember ever meeting Thomas, much less
falling in love with him.
ISBN 978-0-385-74160-6 (hc)—ISBN 978-0-375-98642-0 (ebook)—
ISBN 978-0-375-99013-7 (glb)
1. Memory—Juvenile fiction.   2. Rich people—Juvenile fiction.   3. Paranormal
fiction.   4. New York (N.Y.)—Juvenile fiction.   [1. Supernatural—Fiction.
2. Memory—Fiction.   3. Wealth—Fiction.   4. Love—Fiction.   5. Science
fiction.   6. New York (N.Y.)—Fiction.]   I. Title
PZ7.L4378Mys   2012
813.6—dc23
2012010878

The text of this book is set in 12-point Griffo.

Printed in the United States of America

10 9 8 7 6 5 4 3 2 1

First Edition

For my grandmother,
Eileen Honigman

and

In loving memory of my uncle,
Mark Honigman,
who inspired me with his vast knowledge
of literature and his love of learning,
and who is missed by all

· PROLOGUE ·

So little time is left.

"Take this." He folds the locket into my hand. It throbs as if it has a pulse, giving off a faint white glow. "I'm sorry for putting you in danger."

"I would do it all again," I tell him. "A thousand times."

He kisses me, softly at first, and then so fiercely I can hardly breathe. Rain falls everywhere, soaking us, splashing into the canals that twist through the hot, dark city. His chest heaves against mine. The sound of sirens—and gunshots—reverberates between the crumbling, waterlogged buildings.

My family is drawing closer.

"Go, Aria," he pleads. "Before they get here."

But footsteps are behind me now. Voices fill my ears. Fingers dig into my arms, tearing me away.

"I love you," he says gently.

And then they take him. I scream in defiance, but it is too late.

My father emerges from the shadows. He aims the wicked barrel of his pistol at my head.

Inside me, something bursts.

I always knew this story would break my heart.

PART ONE

But he that dare not grasp the thorn
Should never crave the rose.

—ANNE BRONTË

· I ·

The party has begun without me.

Slowly, I descend the main staircase of our apartment, which curves dramatically into the reception lounge, currently packed with important guests. Tall ceramic vases line the room, overflowing with roses of every variety: white albas from Africa, pink centifolias from the Netherlands, pale yellow tea roses from China, and roses altered with mystic dye right here in Manhattan to produce colors so electric they hardly seem real. Everywhere I turn there are roses, roses, roses—more roses than people.

I reach behind me for assurance. My friend Kiki gives my hand a squeeze, and together we slip into the crowd. I scan the room for Thomas. Where is he?

"I hope your mom doesn't notice we're late," Kiki says, careful not to trample on her dress. Gold, but not garish, her gown falls to the floor in luxurious waves. Her black curls flow past her shoulders in delicate dark loops; both eyelids are dusted with a shimmery pink that makes her brown eyes sparkle.

"She's too busy schmoozing to care," I say. "You look mag, by the way."

"So do you! Shame you're already taken." Kiki eyes the room. "Otherwise, I'd marry you myself."

Practically all the members of the New York State Senate and Assembly are here, as well as our most prominent judges. Not to mention the businessmen and society folk who are indebted to my father, Johnny Rose, or his former political rival, George Foster, for their own success. But tonight isn't about them. Tonight, the spotlight is on me.

"Aria!"

I quickly find the speaker. "Hello, Judge Dismond," I say, nodding to a large woman whose blond hair is swept up into a tornado funnel.

She smiles at me. "Congratulations!"

"Thank you," I say. Since the wedding announcement, the entire city has been celebrating the end of the war between Thomas's and my families, or so I'm told. The *Times* is going to do a profile on me as a political darling and a champion of bipartisan unity—Kiki's been mocking me about it ever since I told her. *My best friend, the darling,* she says in her best phony newscaster voice. I have to cross my eyes and smack her just to get her to stop.

Kiki at my side, I continue my meet-and-greet duties, floating through the party as if I'm on autopilot. "Thank you for coming," I say to Mayor Greenlorn and our state senators, Trick Jellyton and Marishka Reynolds, and their families.

"Quite an engagement party," Senator Jellyton says, raising his glass. "But then, you're quite a girl!"

"You're too kind," I say.

"We were all surprised to hear about you and Thomas Foster," Greenlorn says.

"I am just *full* of surprises!" I laugh, as though I've said something funny. And they all obligingly laugh with me.

I've been groomed for this since I was born—practicing the art of small talk, remembering names, graciously inviting senators' daughters to sleepovers and birthday parties and smiling even when their horrible, zit-faced brothers pretend to bump into me so they can cop a feel. I sigh. Such is the life of a political darling, as Kiki would remind me.

We make our way along the edge of the party, dodging guests and waiters dressed in white who weave through the room carrying trays of hors d'oeuvres and never-ending champagne. I search for Thomas but don't see him.

"Are you excited?" Kiki asks, plucking a miniature lamb burger off one of the trays and popping it into her mouth. "To see Thomas?"

"If by 'excited' you mean 'about to vomit,' then, well, yes."

Kiki laughs, but I'm being serious—I am full of nervous jitters. I haven't seen my fiancé since I woke up in the hospital two weeks ago with partial memory loss. After my accident.

From a distance, the guests seem happy, Rose family cronies mixing easily with Foster devotees. When I look more closely, though, I can see that nearly everyone is shooting nervous, shifty glances around the room, as if the social niceties will be cast aside any second and the families will go back to treating each other as they always have.

As enemies.

My family has despised the Fosters since before my father's father's father was born. Hating them and their supporters is part of what it means to be a Rose.

Or rather, part of what it *meant* to be a Rose.

"Aria?" A young girl rushes up to me. She's around thirteen, with frizzy red hair and a burst of freckles across her forehead. "I just want to say that it's *so* upper about you and Thomas."

"Oh, um . . . thanks?"

She closes in. "How'd you pull off so many secret rendezvous? Is it true that he's moving to the West Side? Do you—"

"Thaaat's enough." Kiki takes over, pushing the girl to the side of the room. "You've got more questions than you do freckles, and that's saying something."

"Who was that?" I ask Kiki once the girl is gone.

"Dunno." Kiki huffs. "Boy, but do they make 'em *small* these days. And round. She was like a little potato. Definitely a Foster supporter."

I frown, curling my fingers into frustrated fists. People I've never even met seem to know every detail of my torrid affair with Thomas Foster, when I can't even remember *meeting* him, let alone falling in love.

When I was released from the hospital and arrived home, I was told of our engagement. I asked my mother why Thomas wasn't at the apartment, why he hadn't visited me in the hospital. "You'll see him soon enough at your engagement party," she said. "The doctors say your memory might still return—perhaps when you see Thomas, it will all come flooding back."

And so here I am. Waiting. Watching for Thomas, so that I can remember.

Kiki must sense that I'm struggling. "Just give it some time, Aria. You loved Thomas enough to defy everything for him—for now, just trust in that."

I nod at her good advice. But *time* is the one thing I don't have. Our wedding is planned for the end of the summer. And it's already almost July.

Guests move all around me, the women swathed in bright colors, parading their jewelry, tattoos, and mystic decals. The men are mostly tall and wide, with rough-looking faces and slicked-back hair.

A distinguished gentleman I don't recognize approaches and extends his hand. His fingers are rough, calloused. "Art Sackroni," he says.

Nod, smile. "Aria Rose."

He is older, with a handsome, weathered face and the black vines of a tattoo creeping up his neck. The Foster family crest—a five-pointed star—is inked in navy blue above his left eye. "I hope you and Thomas will be very happy together, Aria."

"Me too," I say, half meaning it. Two incredibly large men—one black, one white—stand behind him with puffed-out chests, their bow ties looking ready to burst from around their throats. They, too, have tattoos that snake from under their collars.

"It's not every day a young princess finds her prince," Sackroni says.

It sounds corny when he says it like that, but I'm hoping he's right—that once I see Thomas, it will all come rushing back to me and I'll be thrilled to be marrying him instead of terrified.

I think back to when I overdosed on Stic, an illegal drug made of distilled mystic energy. People take it to feel what it is to be a mystic, to experience super speed, incredible strength, a greater harmony with the world, for a fleeting few moments.

I was told that my parents found me unconscious on my bedroom floor, vibrating as if my body were filled with a thousand bees. I can't imagine how I even got hold of the pills. None of my friends use. But I must have gotten them somehow, and leave it to me to screw things up. It's so *embarrassing*. Rich people in the Aeries do Stic all the time. I can't believe I was so stupid—and so unlucky—that the *first* time I tried it I ruined everything.

I remember almost everything else, like what I ate for lunch one day last month (oysters, flown in by my dad from the West Coast) and how it affected me the next morning (two hours hugging the toilet and tossing them all up). So why can't I recall anything about Thomas?

Thankfully, there wasn't any bad publicity. No one outside my immediate family, the Fosters, Kiki, and a handful of doctors and nurses know what happened. Apparently, while I was in the hospital, Thomas came to my parents and confessed that we'd been dating secretly for months. That we wanted to get married.

Now here I am. I should be happy. Overjoyed. But mostly I'm just . . . bewildered, especially about how well my parents took the news.

"There you are," my father says, guiding me toward where my

mother is talking to Kiki. "Claudia, dear," she is saying, "you look gorgeous. Truly ravishing."

"Thank you, Mrs. Rose," Kiki says. "You look stunning, as always."

My mother gives a small, tight smile. Her hair is sculpted into a French twist, her normally blond locks now a mystic-infused scarlet so radiant I nearly have to close my eyes. Her face is slathered in makeup, designed to attract attention and inspire awe.

I look tame compared to her: my makeup is all neutral tones, my brown hair blown out and tucked simply behind my ears.

"You look good, Aria," my father tells me. "Respectable."

I glance down at my dress, the cream-colored silk, the neckline detailed with tiny blue and pink roses, exposing my collarbone and plunging toward my waist in the back. *Of course I look respectable,* I want to say. *I'm a Rose.* But others are watching, so I thank him politely. He nods but doesn't smile. My father never smiles.

My mother's eyes flash around the room, darting over the grand piano and the series of blue period Picassos, past the windows, whose curtains are drawn back to reveal a moonlit city. Then her face lights up and she sings, "Thomas! Over here."

My *fiancé.*

Thomas happens to be gorgeous, with clear tan skin and short brown hair parted on the side. His eyes are dark, like mine, his lips full and inviting. I recognize him immediately from posts on e-columns and pap shots and whatnot, but he's far more striking in person than on any TouchMe screen. He has a magnetic energy. Any girl in all of the Aeries would be thrilled to marry him. He's worth billions, and one day he might even run the city.

My stomach begins to flutter. For a second something tickles the back of my mind: My hand in another person's hand. A pair of lips brushing against mine. A feeling of . . . warmth.

Then it's gone.

Thomas winks at me confidently. Staring at him now, I imagine how I *could* be attracted to him, how I should still *be* attracted to him, even though my memory gives me nothing. And so I pretend: I smile as my parents do, as Thomas does, as our guests do. Because this boy *must* be what I wanted—I defied my family for him, after all.

"Mr. and Mrs. Rose." Thomas shakes my father's hand, lightly kisses my mother's cheek.

It's incredibly disconcerting. When I was little, if I even *said* the name Foster, I was chastised and sent to my room. And now . . .

I exhale a long breath. It's all happening so fast.

"Aria," Thomas says warmly, pecking me on the lips. "How do you feel?"

"Great!" I say, squeezing my clutch and shifting my hands behind my back. They're shaking, and I don't want him to take them in his. "You?"

He narrows his eyes. "Fine. But I wasn't the one who—"

"Overdosed," I reply. "I know."

This is it? Where are all the memories? I was supposed to remember meeting him, falling in love, and . . . Damn. I'm still a blank slate when it comes to Thomas.

My parents exchange a curious glance, no doubt wondering what I'm thinking, but then things get even stranger: Thomas's parents appear.

"Erica! George!" my father says, as though they are his dearest friends. He draws Thomas's father into a masculine hug.

"Everything looks *beautiful*," Thomas's mother says to mine. Erica Foster's dress is an emerald green that matches the dozen or so delicate circles tattooed along her neck. "Absolutely breathtaking."

"Thank you," my mother says with a forced grin.

My father takes a champagne flute from one of the waiters and raises it. "Everyone! Your attention, please."

When my father speaks, people listen. Guests stop talking and turn in our direction. The string quartet stops playing. Thomas slips his arm around my waist, and I am reminded of how oddly we are on display. It's a show for all the most important people in the city, but also—maybe especially—for me.

"It is no secret that George and I have had our differences, and so have our families for generations," Dad says. "But that's all about to change. For the better." There's a quick burst of applause—people know what's coming. "Melinda and I are proud to announce the engagement of our daughter, Aria, to young Thomas Foster. A couple has never been more in love than these two."

There is loud and sustained applause—it goes on just long enough that my father has to fan his right hand to silence everyone. This, too, feels staged. I can feel Thomas's hand on my bare arm. He rubs his thumb along the back of my elbow and my pulse begins to race.

"I'm sure most of you were surprised to hear of the engagement. Initially, Aria and Thomas hid their affair from all of us. But admitting the truth had a positive effect: it forced our two families to . . . rethink our rivalry.

"We decided to bury the hatchet. No more will we fight among ourselves. Aria and Thomas have brought us all together using the oldest power in the book: true love. So, Thomas, thank you. And Aria, my dearest darling daughter, thank you, too." My father kisses me on the forehead. I'm dizzy with the attention.

The applause this time goes on even longer, and it's so strong it pounds against me and Thomas like crashing waves. We link our hands and raise them, inciting the crowd to even louder clapping. Thomas's palm is sweaty.

My father's speech has surprised me. He is a con man and a blackmailer, a leader of thugs. Head of a political party that controls half of Manhattan. To him, love is something you use to manipulate the weak.

But now he is saying that true love trumps all. Ha.

"Which brings me to my next point," my father continues, the applause dying away. "There are enemies out there bigger than either of our families, and the only way to confront them is to follow the lead of these two lovers—to stand united! A radical mystic named Violet Brooks has been gaining power. The poor nonmystic families in the Depths mistakenly think she can offer them higher-paying jobs, and the registered mystics support her for obvious reasons: she's one of them. This woman threatens to destroy everything we've built here in the Aeries. As you know, there hasn't been a third-party mayoral candidate since the Conflagration.

"So tonight, in addition to this engagement, George Foster and

I are announcing our political union. In times of danger and mystic threat, we must all come together. Now that Mayor Greenlorn's term is approaching its end, George and I will both be endorsing *one* candidate in the upcoming election: Garland Foster."

Garland, Thomas's older brother, appears next to us and gives a confident wave. He looks like a more mature version of Thomas, only with blond hair and a thinner and slightly more sinister face. At twenty-eight, Garland is ten years older than Thomas, but he's still quite young for politics. His wisp of a wife, Francesca, stands slightly behind him, a delicate hand on his shoulder.

"So please," my father finishes, "raise your glass and let us drink to the beginning of a new era: for my family, for the Fosters, and for this glorious city!"

The string quartet begins playing again, and my father whirls my mother into the middle of the room, which has been cleared of furniture for the party. George and Erica Foster follow.

My father's words echo in my head: *mystic threat.*

Once lauded for helping to enhance and strengthen our city, mystics are now feared. Uncontrolled, a powerful mystic's touch can kill an ordinary human.

Personally, I don't understand what all the fuss is about. These days, nearly two decades after the Mother's Day Conflagration, the mystic-organized explosion that took so many innocent lives, all mystics are required by law to be drained of their powers twice a year, rendering them harmless. Most live far away from us, among the poor, in the lower level of the city, known as the Depths—a place too terrible and too dangerous for anyone from the Aeries to even visit. The mystics in the Aeries are servants or waiters or government workers who don't care about revolution or power. All they care about is earning enough to survive.

But not all mystics are harmless, I know. There are those who went into hiding, who refused to register with the government and be drained of their magic. Who are lurking in the Depths. Waiting. Hiding. Plotting.

Thomas's arm drops from my waist. "I haven't seen Kyle yet," he says.

"Neither have I." My brother, Kyle, despises the spotlight. Parties are *not* his thing. He's probably holed up somewhere with his girlfriend, Bennie.

"Would you like to dance?" Thomas asks. He looks like he really does want to dance, and too many people are watching for me to say no. I hand my clutch to Kiki and step into the middle of the room.

Thomas's hands are slightly clumsy, as though they're unfamiliar with my body. I suddenly wonder whether we've seen each other naked, and feel my cheeks warm.

"I was really worried about you," he says, rocking us gently back and forth. His cologne smells of cedar and the slightest hint of vanilla. The quartet is playing something beautiful and slow by Górecki. "You hurt yourself so badly."

"Other than some headaches, I feel completely fine." *Except for the fact that you're practically a stranger.* I push that thought away, letting the music fill me. Maybe if I dance long enough, I'll remember what it felt like to dance with Thomas for the first time. Surely we've danced together before? My skin tingles with a feeling I can only call anticipation. Thomas is eligible, handsome, and clearly attracted to me. If I'm as in love with him as everyone says, then I'm quite lucky.

"How did we meet?" I whisper so that no one else can hear.

He pulls back slightly. "You really can't remember anything?"

I shake my head.

Ever since I was a little girl, I have wanted to fall in love. The love you see on TV or read about in books, where you find your missing half—the person you were meant to be with forever—and suddenly you're complete. That's the sort of love my parents say I share with Thomas. Why, then, when he touches me, does it merely feel like a touch?

I thought true love would sear me.

My mother appears, slipping her hand between us. "Aria, I need to borrow your fiancé for a moment. Governor Boch wants to speak with him."

Thomas chastely kisses my forehead. "I'll be back."

I watch them go. Is this what my future with Thomas will be—business, meetings, and our parents? My chest suddenly feels constricted, like my gown is too tight.

I need to get out of here.

I scurry along the far wall and press the panel by the balcony. It reads my biometrics and the door disappears, then reappears behind me. Outside, it's blazing hot. My arms and neck and legs are immediately damp with sweat.

The heat, they say, is because of the global climate crisis, the melting of snow and ice around the world and the rising sea level that swallowed Antarctica and all of Oceania'. Global warming is also to blame for the canals that line the Depths, filling what used to be low avenues and streets with seawater. Soon, the scientists say, the rising waters will overtake the entire island.

No one knows exactly how soon *soon* is.

I walk forward to the edge of the balcony. Before me is all of the Aeries, so high above the surrounding water it sometimes feels like a city afloat, not even tethered to the earth. A few dozen stories below me are the light-rails; sleek white cars blink in and out of stations, bright blurs between the shadows of the skyscrapers. The skyline is jagged and spectacular, illuminated by the city's mystic light posts: super-tall glass spires full of the mystic energy that fuels all of Manhattan—the only useful thing about those freaks, my father always says.

The spires pulse and glow; there seems to be a rhythm to the way they brighten and fade, a kind of visual music. They almost look alive—more alive, anyway, than the guests here tonight.

I carefully roll up the hem of my dress, step on the iron railing, and then swing myself over. I've done this before, a dozen times when I was younger. It relaxes me. The wind tosses my hair and I can barely see, my hands tight on the railing behind me. Slowly, I lean out, the canals thin ribbons of silver in the darkness below me, the hot wind buffeting me until I am reminded: I fought for true love, and I won.

Now I just have to remember it.

I picture Thomas grabbing my hand, Thomas catching me as I run into his arms, Thomas kissing me in dark corners or in light-filled solariums, but it just doesn't compute. I glance back at the party. From here, it's just a jostle of dark suits and bright dresses, barely visible through the condensation on the glass doors.

Behind me, the updraft catches my skirt, and I laugh as the material billows around me. Enough. Time to climb back onto the balcony, where it's safe.

This is when I see him—a face in the corner that startles me.

I can't tell who he is; the light from the wall sconces barely reaches him. "Hello?" I call. "Who's there?"

I've started to bring my leg back over the railing when my other foot slips.

And just like that, I'm falling.

There is the sharp pain of my knee cracking against the ledge, my chin hitting the railing, my body slipping heavily backward. At last I catch a railing with one hand and clutch it tightly.

My body slams against the building's side and I almost let go, but no: I am suspended over the city. I squeeze tighter. Only my five fingers clenched around an iron bar are saving me from plunging thousands of feet to my death.

I feel sweat slicking my palms, my grip loosening. My heart pumps ferociously and I pray silently, *Please don't let me die. Please don't let me die.*

Then the boy is there. I am crying and my vision is blurry, and it's as if he is there but also not there, like a ghost.

"Grab my hand," he says, lowering his arm.

"I can't! I'll fall."

"I won't let you," he tells me. I blink away my tears but I still can't see his face. I hear the sound of his breath, his exasperation, his fear. "You have to trust me."

With one hand still around the iron bar, I swing the other toward the mysterious boy. He catches it and pulls me up, but my legs still dangle below the ledge. His touch feels incredibly warm, like his fingertips are going to scorch my skin.

"Good," he says. "Now the other."

"I don't think I can," I say. My whole body is aching.

"You're stronger than you think," he says.

I will myself not to look down. I take a deep breath and shift my right hand from the railing into his grip, noticing a starburst tattoo on the inside of his wrist. Then I am up, up, and over.

My feet touch the balcony, and I begin to sob—tears that have been welling in me all night. "Shhh, you're safe. You're okay," he says, and even though it's a billion degrees outside and I've probably ruined my most gorgeous dress, I believe him.

Finally, I feel the pressure of his grasp lighten, and I hear him stepping away. Who is this boy who just saved my life?

I whip my head around, searching for him, but he's gone, as if by magic. I have no clue what he looks like. I never even learned his name.

Just then, a familiar voice calls out. "Aria? Is that you?" It's Kiki.

"What are you doing out here?" she asks, approaching me. "I'm burning up."

I decide to keep what just happened to myself for now. "I was just thinking," I say.

"Well, stop thinking and start dancing! Thomas is looking for you. He says they're playing your song."

"We have a song?" I ask stupidly.

"Apparently. Come on," Kiki says, handing me back my clutch.

I'm almost at the door when I hear a rattling sound and realize that something unfamiliar is *in* the clutch. I open it and peer inside—it's a locket I've never seen before. Silver and shiny, but there's something old-looking about it. I take it out and feel a jolt of energy run through me. A memory, a feeling, flashes in my head: this locket is mine.

There is a tiny piece of paper inside the clutch, too. I unfold it. Written in handwriting I do not recognize is one word:

Remember

· II ·

The next morning I wake before Davida comes to help me bathe and dress. My chin is sore from last night's fall, and my knees are bruised, but otherwise, I'm fine. More than fine, actually—I'm elated to feel something besides a crippling sense of memory loss.

Thomas.

I've been taught my entire life to despise him, but he actually seems . . . nice. Concerned. Sensitive. Maybe if my memory *doesn't* return, I could learn to love him all over again.

I roll out of bed and splash water on my face in the bathroom. Luckily, I've been endowed with my mother's dewy skin and my father's big brown eyes. As I purse my lips in the mirror, I have to admit I look pretty good for a girl who almost died.

I find my clutch and shake out the locket, turning it over in my hands. Nothing about it seems extraordinary. It is smooth, for the most part, with tiny grooves in a sort of swirling pattern. No clasp. It's completely solid.

Maybe it's not a locket at all, just a seamed heart.

I take out the note. Stare at it for a moment. Then I drop the locket and the note back into my clutch, closing them away in my armoire. *Remember. . . .*

Then I sit down with my TouchMe. My parents took it away after my overdose but gave it back to me last night before the party.

I scroll through the various applications to my email. I search for "locket," but nothing comes up. Then I search the messages by date, starting with the most recent ones. A few congratulatory notes regarding graduation and the engagement, but that's it— nothing from Thomas or Kiki or any of the other girls at Florence Academy who graduated with me about two months ago. And there are no texts whatsoever—the memory is almost completely blank.

There's a knock on my door. Davida. I cross the room, my feet sinking into the soft gray carpet, and press the touchpad.

"May I come in?" she asks as the door retracts.

"Of course," I say, and put my TouchMe down. Davida is, as usual, in her uniform of all black: long-sleeved blouse with a dramatic collar, tapered pants tucked into well-polished shoes with no heels, thin black gloves.

The gloves are her personal touch. She has always worn them—since she was eleven, anyway. That was when she suffered a tragic cooking accident at the orphanage where she grew up. I've never seen her hands, but Kyle gave me nightmares when I was younger by imagining what they must look like: *scar tissue halfway to her elbows, the skin marbled and stiff and shiny, like the hands of a movie monster.*

"You're up early," Davida says. Her dark hair is pulled back into an impeccable bun. At seventeen, exactly my age, Davida has the kind of face girls dream of having—wide hazel eyes, high cheekbones, lips that dominate the lower half of her face. Unlike most people in the Aeries, my parents refuse to employ mystics; Davida and the others in our household are all members of the nonmystic lower class. "Magdalena has started a pot of coffee if you'd like some."

Magdalena mostly serves my mother, and she brews the darkest coffee of any of our help—too dark for me. "No thank you, Davida."

I watch as Davida goes to make my bed. She leans down and picks up the end of the comforter with one hand, straightening it with her gloved fingers. "How are you feeling?"

I've heard that question so many times lately that it makes me want to scream. Coming from Davida, though, it's a relief. Technically, she's my servant, but we've never had a formal relationship. Being the same age, we grew close quickly. We're friends. My parents haven't minded that we get along or that we spend time together, as long as she does her work and knows her role in the household. "I'm not sure. I *feel* fine physically, but, well . . . I'm a bit jumbled up."

Davida squints at me. "What happened to your chin?"

I'm about to tell her about my fall when I notice that the glove of her right hand has left sooty prints on my comforter. She sees them, too, and tries to slap the soot away.

Odd. Davida is never anything but pristine. There's something she's not telling me, and soot like that can only come from one place. "Davida, were you in the Depths?"

Just then, my mother strolls in. "Good morning, Aria," she says. "Davida."

Davida straightens. "Good morning, Mrs. Rose."

"Is it?" my mother asks. Her voice is particularly grating today. "Aria, I'm so disappointed in you. We're lucky the Fosters had too much champagne to notice your behavior last night."

"Me? What did I do?"

"You went outside on the balcony and ignored people."

"Only for a few minutes—"

"This was your engagement party! Acting distant only makes people think you don't want to get married."

"I thought I was acting nice," I tell her, "but if I was acting distant . . . maybe it is because I still don't remember Thomas. I've told you this. You can understand why I might be a little shy."

My mother perches on the edge of my bed and stares at me intently. I'm tired of constantly having to prove my worth, my devotion to the family and to our political ambitions. I always come up short.

"How am I supposed to marry Thomas if I don't even know him?"

My mother waves her hand in the air. "Nonsense, Aria. You *love* him. You snuck around with him in the Depths, betrayed everything our family stood for, and risked your father's anger—and our downfall. It's a shame your own poor decisions have confused what you were obviously once so passionate about."

I'm immediately ashamed. My love for Thomas *must* have been strong. The Depths are a wild, dark place. Going there is dangerous. I wouldn't have risked my life for just anyone.

"Really, though, what's the harm in pushing back the wedding—even just another month?" I ask tentatively. "Maybe my memory will return by then."

My mother's lips tighten, and she says her next words slowly. "Your father and I have done everything possible to help you regain your memory—consulted specialists, procured off-the-market pharmaceuticals. I know it's only been two weeks, but we're trying, and there is more than just your feelings at stake."

Two weeks is not a long time, I want to say, but it doesn't matter. The message is clear: it doesn't matter that I don't remember. I'm marrying Thomas no matter what—and it feels like a death sentence.

"Maybe if I just talk to Thomas, have some time alone with him . . ."

"You *had* time with him, Aria," my mother says. "Last night."

"We weren't alone! That was a *huge* party." If I snuck around in the Depths with him, and they've accepted that, why can't I see him alone now?

"Once you're *married* . . . you can spend as much time with Thomas as you like. Until then, focus on getting better." My mother claps her hands together, and her scowl is replaced by a sunny smile. "You have a doctor's appointment tomorrow, darling," she says, and she sounds like a warmer mother. "We'll be sure to tell him that your memory loss has yet to improve. We all want you to remember Thomas."

She kisses me on the forehead and leaves.

I try not to cry. I *will* remember.

Davida rests a hand on my shoulder. "Come," she says. "Let's get you dressed."

Kiki arrives a few hours later to take me out to lunch. We're meeting up with my brother's girlfriend, Bennie Badino, then attending a plummet party.

"Can I tag along?" Kyle asks, splayed out across a couch in the living room.

"Absolutely not," says Kiki, who is standing impatiently in the kitchen, a Slagger purse dangling from her elbow. She's wearing a knee-length skirt the color of ripe tangerines; her sleeveless beige top is tight across her chest, with a low V-neck. "It's a girls' lunch. If you came with us, it would be . . . a girls' lunch plus a boy."

"I can be a girl," Kyle says. "I'll just pretend to have no common sense and cry all the time for no reason."

"I don't mind if he comes," I tell her, smoothing out my skirt. Kyle and I haven't spent a lot of time together recently—at twenty, he lives at the university during the year, and is only home for the summer.

Kiki throws her arms up. "Doesn't anyone care about the sanctity of feminine bonding over expensive salads?" She stamps her foot. "I refuse!"

"Fine, fine." Kyle gets up from the sofa and runs a hand through his hair. Unlike mine, his complexion is fair; he has light green eyes, blond hair, pale skin. Almost every girl at Florence Academy has had a crush on him at some point. "I'll ring up Danny and ask him to eat with me. And then when you try to come over and hang out with us, we won't let you. Boys only. See how you like it."

"We'll like it just fine," Kiki says, then turns to me. "Now come on. We're going to be late meeting Bennie if we don't leave *now.*" She rushes over to Kyle, kissing him once on each cheek. "It's what they do in Europe," she says. "My mother just got back from Italy. All they do there is kiss on each cheek and eat spaghetti. Anyway, ciao!"

We exit the building and cross the arched bridge that links our skyscraper with the next, then another bridge to the nearest light-rail station. There are stations throughout the Aeries. They're all oversized rectangular buildings made of reflective glass to help block heat from the sun.

Kiki and I step inside—unlike the air outside, it's ice cold in here.

"Come on, Aria. Keep up!"

The station entrance opens into a large waiting area, where people are milling about, meeting friends on incoming cars or simply seeking respite from the heat. On either side of the station is a wall of terminals—one for cars heading uptown, another for cars heading downtown—and lines of people. The lines can get quite long, but the light-rail moves so quickly that you never have to wait more than a few moments.

"Waiting," Kiki says as we're in line and the light above Terminal Four lights up, indicating it's available, "is never as fun as *not* waiting."

A shuttle blinks in almost immediately.

We walk forward and Kiki presses her hand against the scanner.

flashes on a screen overhead. The doors retract, letting her into the car.

"I do love seeing my name in lights," she says over her shoulder.

The doors remain open as I complete my own scan.

ARIA ROSE

flashes overhead as I enter the car.

"The Circle," Kiki announces to the car's autopilot. She plops down on one of the cushioned seats. I sit, too. Even though the rail is incredibly smooth—it barely feels like we're moving at all—I've sometimes gotten nauseated when I look outside the glass and see the city flashing by.

A few minutes later, the doors open at the Circle, the complex of stores and restaurants around Fifty-Ninth Street on the West Side, which we love to frequent. Everything is enclosed in a large glass dome to keep out the hot air, the buildings connected by tiny bridges with mystic slidewalks that move beneath your feet.

When we were younger, Kyle and I would come to the Circle and just stand still, letting the pavement shuffle us all around the inside of the dome. We would look at the shops and smell the food, content simply to watch. These days all we do is see each other on the way in and out of the apartment, if that. We barely even text.

Now, Kiki and I bypass all the stores and head straight to the American, which is the perfect venue for a plummet party. Made entirely of glass, the circular dining room provides a panoramic view of Manhattan, and when you're there in the evening, all you see is blackened sky.

Just as we're about to enter, I turn to Kiki. "Did you happen to notice if one of the guests at the party last night had a starburst tattoo?"

"Hmmm?" Kiki says, half listening and fixing her hair.

"A boy . . . well, someone our age. Who might've had a tattoo on his wrist. Did you see anyone like that?"

"No," Kiki says, shaking her head. "But I wish I had. Sounds hot."

Inside, we're greeted immediately and taken to the front of the line.

"Ah, Ms. Rose," says the host, a young man with spiky black hair. "So good to see you again."

"You too, Robert."

"You must come more often. Congratulations on the engagement." He beams at me. "May I see it?"

"See what?" Kiki asks.

"The ring, of course," Robert says.

I glance at my hands, which are completely bare. Engagement ring. I can't remember ever having one, and yet . . . this seems like such an important detail. I'm surprised my mother didn't make an issue of my not wearing one last night.

"Is our table ready?" Kiki asks, thankfully changing the subject.

"Follow me," Robert says with a bow. "Your other guest is already seated."

I hear Bennie before I see her. "Ladies! You look gorgeous!" Bennie is tall, with legs that go on forever. She has black, shoulder-length hair and skin the color of the caramels I used to eat when I was younger. She's three years older than me—Kyle's age—and while she's not conventionally beautiful, she has a certain spark that draws people. A brazen confidence, a sense of adventure. Plus, she shares my taste in music: bands with boys who sing about broken hearts. Of all the girls my brother has dated, I like her the most.

"Thank you, darling," Kiki says. We exchange a round of kisses and sit down. "I feel more plucked than a chicken," she continues. "I went to the dermatologist this morning and got a pore zap."

Immediately, two waiters—servants from the Depths—fill our water glasses. Etiquette dictates that we not speak to them. As a child, I used to feel guilty about letting Depthshods serve us. I remember once when I was ten, thanking a waiter—both of us were slapped by my mother as a result. I haven't risked it since.

"A pore zap?" Bennie asks skeptically. "I've never heard of that."

"Me either," I say.

"I'm not surprised." Kiki looks around the room as though she suspects someone of eavesdropping. "They're very experimental. I could have dropped dead then and there." She smacks the table. "That's the price we pay for beauty, girls!"

"But what *is* it?" Bennie asks, leaning forward.

Kiki shakes her head. "Sorry, Bennie. Love ya, but you've got butter lips. Can't keep a secret. Once I tell you what a pore zap is, the entire Aeries will know, and then everyone will look as good as I do and I'll have no chance of getting a boyfriend, which defeats the whole purpose of getting a pore zap in the first place."

"Hey!" Bennie says. "I resent that. I do not have . . . butter lips."

"They're so buttery I could rub a piece of bread on them and I'd have myself a meal," Kiki says.

Bennie gasps. "You're so full of—"

"Ladies," I interject, "what is everyone going to eat?" I glance down; each table setting has a menuscreen to touchpad your order. I quickly choose a chicken salad and change the subject, asking Kiki what on earth happened to my engagement ring while Bennie ponders the menu.

"It's being engraved," she says. "Thomas mentioned it last night. Didn't anyone tell you?"

"Oh. No, but that makes sense." I feel relieved. A simple answer.

"If I'd actually known you were even dating, I could have told you that a while ago," Kiki says. "But you're the lady with the secrets." Her voice is tinged with disappointment. She's mad at me for keeping my relationship with Thomas from her, and I understand her frustration.

"I'm sorry, Kiks. If I could remember *why* I didn't tell you, well . . . I'd tell you. But I don't. Don't be mad, please?"

She sighs, scrolling through the touchpad and ordering her lunch. "Fine, whatever. I'm hungry. Should I get the squid? Is squid good?" She presses down with her thumb. "I guess I'll find out!"

Hearing about my engagement ring leads me to think about another piece of jewelry: the locket. Perhaps Kiki knows something about that as well. I catch her gaze. "Did Thomas ever buy me a locket?"

"What's with you and all the questions today? I don't know. Maybe."

"Think," I say. "Bennie, do you remember seeing me with a locket? An older-looking thing shaped like a heart? Vintage?"

Bennie shakes her head.

"Thomas has bought you a ton of presents, I'm sure," Kiki says. "What do you care about some old locket?"

I don't know what to say without revealing too much. The mysterious locket, the cryptic note—surely they are pieces of a puzzle, but I have no clue how to put them together.

"Never mind," I reply. "Just wondering."

The food comes quickly, and the three of us do what we do best: eat and gossip. Bennie wants to know more about the party, since she spent most of it upstairs in Kyle's arms. She's in her third year with Kyle at West University, where all the Rose supporters go. Kiki and I have both been accepted to West, too. Typically, after graduating from high school, people from the Aeries take a year to travel and see the world before entering college.

I'm going to be a wife.

Despite that realization, I find the conversation comfortable, familiar, just as it always was before the overdose, and I'm grateful for it.

And then it's time.

We push aside our plates and stand with everyone else, then are directed to the opposite side of the dining area, which has been roped off. Servers hand out glasses of champagne as people take their spots before the windows.

The plummet party is about to begin.

Because of global warming and the seawater that fills Manhattan's depths, the foundations of the city are eroding. Every year, certain buildings are deemed unsafe because of water damage belowground— to the cement, the soil, to whatever it is skyscrapers rest on. The condemned buildings are abandoned, and a team of demolition experts guides the wreckage straight down so that no one is hurt. At first, these occurrences were feared by those in the Aeries; now, however, they're celebrated.

Really, they're almost beautiful to watch: the corner of a skyscraper suddenly sinks and the building contorts with a low shriek of metal, windows shattering as the stresses reshape the walls and floors. Then the upper floors accordion down to the waters below.

By the time a plummet begins, everyone in the building has already fled to safety—but not always. Sometimes a sinking comes on suddenly, and then workers rush in and try to support the building while rescuers empty the floors.

They don't always arrive in time.

The building we're losing today has been around for over a century, a tall black skyscraper with a mirrored front.

"What do you think happens when the building actually sinks?" I ask.

Kiki rolls her eyes. "It goes into the ocean, silly."

"That's not what I mean." I glance around the restaurant. People are chatting idly, waiting for the party to begin. What must it be like to witness a plummet from below, to live in a world where it rains granite and glass?

"Well, then what?" Bennie asks.

I think for a second. "Everything happens so smoothly from way up here. I wonder what it's like in the Depths. If things get . . . messy."

"Who cares?" Kiki says, shrugging as a trio of girls move past us. "Hey, isn't that Gretchen Monasty?"

"What is she doing here?" Bennie hisses. "She should stay on her own side."

I blink. Gretchen Monasty—her family is a huge supporter of the Fosters. She's pretty, I suppose, with sleek brown hair, almond-shaped eyes, and a nose that scoops to a pointed tip. I've seen her picture on tons of gossip blogs; she's quite the socialite. I'm surprised she's here, but since Thomas and I are getting married, I suppose the decades-old boundaries that divide Manhattan into East and West sides no longer matter.

"Calm down," I say. "It's no big deal."

Even though it sort of is.

A bell rings. Everyone quiets, and Kiki and Bennie and the rest of the crowd gaze out the window at the building that's about to fall. I, however, can't stop staring at Gretchen. I remember my mother's words this morning, and I know what a Rose daughter should do.

"Excuse me"—I lean past Kiki and hold out my hand—"we haven't met, but I thought I would say hello. These are my friends—Bennie Badino and Kiki Shoby." I smile as genuinely as possible. "I'm Aria Rose."

One of the girls standing next to Gretchen—with stringy hair and milky eyes—leans forward. "We know who you are," she says.

Then Gretchen's other friend finishes her sentence: "And frankly, we're not impressed. Don't you think some things should remain how they were—separate? My parents don't like yours for a reason."

The bell rings again and the top part of the building folds in on itself like it's made of soggy paper. Even from inside the restaurant, the noise is tremendous—a harsh shrieking of metal and stone, bending and scraping, the vibrating booms of the floors falling atop one another like heavy rocks banging underwater.

My smile fades. "Excuse me?"

Before us is a cloud of atomized rubble, a dusty billowing where the building used to be. Once the smoke clears, nothing is there anymore. Just a hole in the skyline, like a missing tooth.

I expect Gretchen to apologize for her friend's inexcusable behavior. Instead, she stares at me with disgust. "Thomas was right about you."

Gretchen has hit me right where it hurts: the fiancé I can't remember.

Kiki pipes up, her face beet-red. "I. Have. Never," she says, "witnessed such rudeness from such hideous girls in my entire seventeen years on this spinning planet. You have some nerve." She wags a finger in Gretchen's face and says, "Some nerve." Then she turns to me and says, "Let's go, Aria."

Bennie, who has remained silent this entire time, follows Kiki as she pushes past the rows of people. I trail behind them, focused on Gretchen's mouth, which is wide open. Meanwhile, the building is gone. Everyone around me is applauding wildly, overjoyed by how quickly something can disappear. Am I the only one who wishes things would come *back*?

Later that evening, I stare out the windows in my bedroom. It's dark, and the city lights sparkle like jewels. The sky is midnight blue and streaked with smoky wisps of clouds. The hint of a moon reflects off the silvery webs of the nearby bridges and terminals.

I know I won't be able to sleep. I can't get Gretchen Monasty out of my head, the snotty tone of her voice: *Thomas was right about you.*

Right about what? Was she talking about the overdose or something else?

The locket. The note. Maybe Thomas knows something that can help me, something he hasn't been able to tell me in front of my parents, or his.

I should ask him. I grab my TouchMe, about to call him, when I realize I don't have his number. Odd. Unless I was worried about my parents finding it, so I never put it in there to begin with. I think for a minute. It's not like any of my friends would have his number. Plus—like me and my parents—I'm sure he's unlisted.

I want to pull out my hair or scream in frustration. But neither of those things will solve my problems or bring my memory back.

On the surface, my story is a simple one. I fell in love. I took a drug. I had a bad reaction, and I'm suffering some temporary memory loss as a result.

But if I really think about it . . . there are so many things that don't make sense, questions that beg to be asked and answered— most of which involve Thomas.

I listen quietly, hearing nothing in my apartment. It's just after ten-thirty at night; my parents must be asleep, the servants turned in. I glance back outside, at the starless sky. On the East Side, across the city, my fiancé is probably in his bedroom—and he may very well have a clue to help unlock my past.

The answer, I realize, is simple: I must go to him.

· III ·

Escape is not easy.

A simple fact: every fingertouch scanner that operates every door in all of the Aeries is hooked up to an electronic security grid. The west side of that grid is overseen by my father's security entourage. A system monitors the location of every individual, and the central operators are alerted when certain people of high status—myself included—make a move.

Because the Grid is watched so closely, I'm able to travel around the Aeries without bodyguards. I had them when I was little, but when I turned sixteen, my father granted me my freedom. Or at least, as much freedom as you can have when you're constantly being monitored.

"A true Rose can fend for herself," he told me. Though I'm sure he regretted those words when I started sneaking around with Thomas. Whenever that was.

Just before my accident, Kyle let it slip that the back elevator in our kitchen operates without a fingertouch—it just requires a passcode, which he gave me—and that it goes directly to the sub-entry level of the building. My father and his associates use it when they want their illicit activity to remain off the Grid.

Which is exactly how I want my activity to remain tonight.

Wearing the cloak Davida gave me for my birthday last year, I move slowly down the stairs, across the main floor of our apartment, and into the back elevator. I hold my breath as the door closes.

When it opens, I'm in an eerily bright room—the service entrance. The floor is pristine silver save for a black path that leads outside. I tread softly, hoping there aren't any invisible sensors or hidden cameras. I wait for an alarm to sound, or the security guards to burst in and stop me.

Nobody does.

Outside, I start sweating before I've even crossed the narrow bridge that connects our building to its neighbor. I keep to the shadows as I hurry past the light-rail station, its glass roof shining brightly against the black-blue sky. I can't use the rail. It tracks passengers. Instead, I must take the long way to the East Side to ensure that my father isn't notified of my whereabouts.

A few blocks down is a Point of Descent. While light-rails operate solely in the Aeries, PODs are like elevators to the Depths. Nobody we know uses PODs, only the Depthshod and the mystics who work in the Aeries. Why would anyone ever want to go down to the canal levels unless they absolutely *had* to?

But that snobbery is something I can use to my advantage: PODs run an oldware version of fingertouch—slow, outmoded technology that doesn't interface well with the new software in the Aeries. So it's less likely anyone will be able to track me.

I place my hand on the scanner and am cleared.

The inside of the POD is much dirtier than I imagined. Fortunately, I don't have much time to inspect it closely before we descend.

Despite having lived in Manhattan my entire life, I have only been to the Depths once before, on a closely monitored field trip with the Florence Academy. I remember the awful stench, the people with no homes to call their own and no food to fill their bellies. Everything and everyone was dirty and undesirable. We were told that the Depths were full of people who'd murder us for whatever we had in our pockets.

Leaving the POD, I realize that the Depths are exactly how I remember them: sticky-hot, loud, dangerous. Water gently laps at the foundations of the buildings, a constant sound track as I walk along the raised sidewalks. I move past a row of crumbling brownstones and shops, their windows caked with so much grime I can't even see a hint of my reflection. Everything is darker down here. I don't know where I'm going, but I try my best to not look suspicious. Swarms of people move past, their faces hidden by mist rising from the warm canal water that fills the streets.

I can practically taste the salt water in the suffocating air. Folks pass me by, chatting in loud voices, oblivious to my presence. There's something undeniably exciting about it all—being somewhere I'm not supposed to be late at night, seeing real people live their lives without them noticing me.

Blending in feels good.

A hunchbacked woman with frazzled hair approaches me.

"Spare a few pennies, miss?" I take out some change and drop it into her creased palm.

It feels odd to have real money. Everything in the Aeries is paid for by finger scan, billed directly to the bank. Luckily, I've come prepared, taking a stash of coins I've collected over the years.

I come upon a slight hill, where the old street rises out of the waters and is walkable. I step over a black garbage bag onto the pavement, then cross to the water's edge, where gondoliers sit patiently in their boats, smoking and waiting for customers.

Years ago, the government installed motorized gondolas in the canals. They're operated by gondoliers; this is how most people get around in the Depths. Once I'm on the East Side, I'll ascend via POD and then find a way into Thomas's residence. I may not know his phone number, but the Fosters' home address is common knowledge.

The only real problem is what to say once I'm there. "Why did you talk about me with Gretchen?" is too accusatory, while "Tell me everything you know about what happened to me" is too . . . demanding. I have to play this just right.

But if Thomas knows something, and he loves me, why *wouldn't* he want to help?

A few girls my own age rush past, laughing and calling out. They wear simple dresses of gray and dirty white and washed-out navy. I can tell by their healthy coloring that they're not mystics— rather, they're members of the lower class who live in the Depths. New York City's poor and downtrodden, a population of millions whose votes my parents have never cared about before and now, thanks to Violet Brooks, are terrified of losing.

"How much?" one asks a gondolier.

"Where ya going?"

"East," the girl says. "To Park." The gondolier holds up his hand and flashes all five fingers. The girls hop aboard.

I motion for a gondolier, then gingerly navigate the broken pavement. Careful not to fall into the water, I climb into one of the boats and sit. My skin feels like it might boil, it's so hot; I want to remove my cloak entirely, but I'm too afraid I'll be recognized and reported.

"Where to, miss?" The gondolier looks young—not much older than me—with a sweet face and messy red hair.

"East," I say, just like the girl. "Seventy-Seventh and Park."

He nods and starts up the gondola. There are no oars or paddles, only a tiny electronic wheel. It takes a few moments for us to clear the gondolas ahead, but then we're moving swiftly along the canals and twisting through the Depths. I peer over the side and watch the murky water. It looks far from refreshing: dirty greenish-brown, with a sour smell that turns my stomach.

Noise carries over the canals as we motor along—laughter, music, yelling that alarms me at first but that I gradually realize is coming from a game between two young boys on the street.

"Kids," the gondolier says with a chuckle. "Never a quiet moment."

I can barely hear him over the motorized hum. The gondolier seems nice—young.

We round a corner, and the water-filled canyons between the

buildings suddenly open out into a wide expanse of blue-black sky. The Magnificent Block, I remember from that long-ago field trip. This is the area where the registered mystics are forced to live. In truth, the Block is far from magnificent—dark and dreary, with flimsy-looking tenements one on top of another like stacks of playing cards, peeking out from behind a stone enclosure.

Years ago, this place was called Central Park. I've seen tons of pictures of when it was lush and green and filled with trees. People would come here from every corner of Manhattan to play and picnic and escape the city. But that was before global warming, before the seas rose and hid the park under thirty feet of dirty water. Before it was designated a reservation for mystics and walled off. The parts that remain above water are spectacularly dingy but pretty much invisible to the rest of the city, thanks to the high stone walls and rusty-looking gates that seal off the area.

The divide is quite clear: mystics inside the Block, everyone else outside.

Once we're past the Block, the buildings rise again, and after we cross a few more streets, the gondolier pulls up alongside a raised sidewalk. He loops a rope over a post and draws the boat in so that it gently scrapes the walkway.

"Here, miss," he says. I hand him some coins and he helps me from my seat.

The night air is darker now, save for a soft twilight glow from the numerous mystic spires in the city. I stay to the shadows, where my face will be difficult to see. Those in the Depths hate the Roses *and* the Fosters. Many of them would love to see me dead.

Here on the Foster side of the city, people use strange sidewalks that were built up over the years into steep banks as the waters rose. But the construction was done by citizens, not the city, and the sidewalks are shabby things that are hard to walk on.

I reach Park Avenue and discover that the POD terminal is actually on the other side of the canal. But a short block away there is a footbridge, easy enough to cross. I look up and see the bright towers: the Foster residence. I'm just about to climb the steps of the bridge when I am cut off by a group of wild teens.

There are four boys—all broad-shouldered and thick, dressed in grays and blacks—and two girls standing off to the side, nearly invisible in the shadows of a crumbling abandoned building. Their faces have a pale, hollowed-out look, all sunken cheeks and waxy skin, as if they haven't eaten for days.

The faded awning over their heads reads BROWERS. A storefront of some kind, though judging from the spiderwebs of shattered glass that were the shop windows, this store hasn't been open for years.

The tallest boy, who has rust-colored hair and dull eyes, sneers, "What are ye looking at?" He steps closer, and the other boys close in behind me. The girls just stare.

"You mute?" another boy asks. They all start to laugh. I think again about how people in the Depths would be happy to see me and my family dead, and my hands shake.

"I'd like to pass by, please," I say, trying to sound polite. I realize immediately that *polite* is wrong. *Polite* marks me as someone from the Aeries.

"'Pass by'?" the tall boy repeats in a high-pitched voice. He guffaws. "What are ye here for? Stic?" He pulls out a vial filled with electric green pills. "Good stuff. Promise. Fifty for two."

Stic. Part of me is curious about the pills. I want to see what one looks like up close; maybe it will help revive my memory. But I don't trust these boys.

"No," I reply. Screw polite. I need to sound tough. "Now let me by."

One of the boys moves to the right. In my rush to pass them, the hood of my cloak falls away just as a nearby spire pulsates with energy. The light illuminates my face, and the two girls let out gasps.

"Aria Rose!" one of them says.

"This is so upper," the other one whispers. "No freaking way."

"No, you're mistaken," I say, pulling my hood back up.

"I'd recognize you anywhere." She calls to one of the boys. "Darko!"

I hurry up the stairs, but it's too late: someone rushes up behind me. My cloak is yanked off and the boys surround me.

"Look what we got here," the little one called Darko says. He nudges the tall one with his elbow, then grins. "Isn't it past your bedtime, sweetheart? Does Daddy know you're down below?"

I reach for my cloak, but he tosses it to one of the girls, who squeals and drapes it around her shoulders. "Oh, look at me," she says to the other one, "I'm Aria Rose. Aren't I glamorous with all my fancy threads?"

"Let me," the other girl says, ripping the cloak from her friend. "Ooh la la! I'm Aria Rose. So pretty. So important. Blah blah barf."

They all laugh. I try to stay cool, but everything inside me is screaming that something awful is about to happen. "Very funny," I say. "Now will you let me through? I'm late. Someone . . . People are waiting for me. They'll come looking for me soon."

" 'People'?" Darko asks, baring his teeth. "Like your fiancé? Do you know what a rat he is? What animals they *all* are?"

The tall boy grabs my wrist. "Your families are the reason my parents don't have money. Why we barely have food." He takes something long and silver from within his shirt. "Ever hurt because you're so hungry? Know how painful that is?"

I try to whip away, but two of the other boys hold me still. Slowly, the tall boy turns over my arm. He skims the jagged piece of metal over the pink skin that runs from my elbow to my wrist, letting the edge hover over one of my veins. I am trembling now.

"Please," I say.

He licks his lips with his thick, wet tongue. "Please what?"

"Please don't hurt me."

He tilts his head, looking almost puzzled. Then he plunges the metal deep into my arm.

I cry out, watching as my blood spills down my arm, pooling red in my palm.

He yanks out the metal and holds it up to the light. My blood is black along its edge. "Oops," the boy says, laughing. "Must have slipped."

I close my eyes, willing the pain to stop. I am going to die here. I am going to die for my stupidity.

A rush of wind hits my cheeks.

I open my eyes, and everything before me is different.

The tall boy who shivved me drops to the ground, and the pressure that was on my arms is gone. A ray of green light whizzes by me, nearly two feet long and as narrow as one of my fingertips. The light cleaves the air with a whoosh, and a high-pitched ting fills my ears.

Then I see a second ray of light, identical to the first. It connects forcefully with the neck of one of the other boys, the one with rust-colored eyes, who blows back and falls to the pavement.

This is when I realize that the rays of light are attached to a boy. They must be some sort of mystic energy—which means this is a rebel mystic. Someone who has not registered with the government, who has illegally retained his powers.

The girls back away and turn; I can hear their shoes clobber the pavement as they run. Then I hear the zip of the mystic's rays, so green they're nearly blinding. The mystic whips around me, shielding me from Darko, who has picked up the fallen shiv and is waving it aimlessly through the air.

"Fight like a man, not a freak!" Darko yells.

The mystic just laughs and thrusts his arms into the air. The rays channel into the sky, braiding together from each finger into two thicker beams, one from each hand, like swords of light, wider at the base and sharp at the tip. The pulsing color ignites the sky, casting a greenish glow on Darko and the remaining boy and the lifeless audience of buildings around us.

I am spellbound. I nearly forget that my arm is bleeding. The scene is so magnificent that even Darko stops his slashing and looks up.

This is when the mystic strikes.

In an instant, he cuts the beams from the sky to the ground. The sound they make reminds me of when Kyle and I were younger and used to catch fireflies on the roof, cupping them in our hands and holding them up to our ears. The buzzing is so loud it seems to fill the Depths.

Darko is blasted in the chest. He's tossed nearly ten feet into the air, his arms and legs moving wildly. Then he falls, and I hear the sickening crack of bones.

The remaining boy has a look of horror on his face. He starts to run, but the mystic strikes him in the back—there's a thunderous clap when the green beam finds its target, and the boy flops onto the street.

It's only then that I realize I've been holding my breath. I exhale deeply, filling my lungs, and cast my gaze on the mystic, whose rays have retracted and who is standing in the middle of the street with his hands tucked casually in his pockets.

As if he were anyone. As if he were normal.

Rebel mystics are outlaws. They're dangerous and are to be reported immediately. I know this from a thousand public service announcements I've seen all my life. But . . .

This mystic saved my life.

After a moment, he looks at me and says, "Are you all right?" His voice is deep and smooth as syrup.

I'm shocked by how handsome he is. Clear blue eyes—not as dark as the ocean, but deeper than the sky. Hair that looks touched by the sun, with hints of darker streaks. Thick eyebrows. A straight nose. A square, solid jaw.

"I'm hurt," I manage to say, suddenly feeling woozy.

"Let me see," he says. "Hold out your arm."

He takes my hand in his. A kind of intoxicating warmth spreads through me.

"Hold still." He touches his fingers to the injury. His hand glows from within, like the inner deep burn of a log pulled from a fire. Its radiance throws everything else into shadow—his bones, his skin, his clothing. For a moment he seems to be made of light.

My skin feels sizzling hot. When he lifts his fingers, I see that the cut has healed. Even the blood is gone.

"I—I—"

He smiles at me. It's a beautiful, soothing smile.

"You're welcome," he says. He brushes some of his hair away from his eyes and wipes sweat from his forehead. Then I hear sirens, and a worried look crosses his face. The bodies strewn on the pavement begin to stir. "We need to get out of here before they wake up. Come with me." He wraps a strong arm around my waist and pulls me to him.

So I do what any girl would do when a gorgeous boy saves her life in the seedy Depths of Manhattan: I let him take me away.

· IV ·

"Large cup. Black."

The waitress nods at the boy, then looks at me. There are no menus here in this tiny shop. It is the kind of place I might have walked right by—inconspicuous and dark on the outside, the words JAVA RIVER pressed into the awning.

Inside, though, it is full of light and sound. A handful of plush blue booths are filled with all kinds of people. Mostly families, but there are a few solos eating pastries and drinking coffee. The walls are a creamy color, covered with framed photographs of mountain ranges.

"The same," I say. The waitress—a blob of a girl with curly black hair and a pierced nostril—nods and ambles away.

I give my attention back to the mystic boy who saved me. "Thank you," I say. "For . . . carrying me."

His face is blank, which makes me feel like an idiot. I haven't been carried by anyone since I was a baby. Certainly not a boy my own age. And certainly not a mystic.

But when he took me in his arms and led me away from that

terrible scene, I had no fight left in me. I simply closed my eyes, rested my head on his shoulder, and relaxed. It felt good to be able to trust someone—if only for the length of a few city avenues.

The mystic is still expressionless. His hood is up, covering his hair, making him look like he's trying to travel incognito. He's not perfect. I can see this now. His nose is slightly crooked, as though he was in a fight and never had a doctor set it properly; an inch-long scar runs just above his left eyebrow. His cheeks are light with stubble. He is rugged-looking, the exact opposite of Thomas, whose hair is always combed, his skin smooth. This mystic boy is something else entirely.

He has the kind of face that takes you by surprise. Earlier, on the street, I thought it was one thing—handsome in a conventional way, like porcelain or the colored diamonds my mother keeps in the Rose family vault. But now I see it is quite the opposite, a face too hard to be pretty, too mysterious. It is the kind of face that sucks you in, makes you want to surrender all that you know, all that you are, just to capture its attention.

It is dangerous, this face, this boy. And not simply because he's a mystic, though that is danger enough.

He already has a hold on me. I'm not sure if it's attraction or fear. Or both.

The mystic looks calm. If I didn't know better, I would never guess that he's just been in a fight. He's wearing a red T-shirt and a pair of jeans, and a blue jacket made out of sweatshirt material. He radiates health—and because of that, he stands out here, among other mystics who have had their powers drained.

Typically, those who've had their energy removed have a sickly look about them that I've noted in pictures and learned about in school, and occasionally seen in person. They're drained, of course, to protect us against another revolt like the Mother's Day Conflagration. Without their energy, they can't hurt anyone, and the people who live in the Aeries are safe.

"Where are we?" I ask.

"Java River," he says, pointing to the wall where the name is painted.

"I know *that*," I say, longing for my lost cloak. I'd hide myself in its folds. No one seems to be paying me much attention, but I feel as though all eyes are on me. On us. Maybe I'm just paranoid. "But where *are* we?" I motion to the window. To what is outside.

He leans back. "Oh. We're near the Magnificent Block," he says casually.

I feel my eyes widen. "We're near the Block?"

"Yeah," he says. "Near. Not *in*. Don't worry, you're safe." He looks at me strangely. "Where did you think we were?"

I can't answer his question, though I certainly didn't think we were so close to the Block. I expected the surrounding area to be a little more . . . run-down, and surprisingly, it's not. The people here look a lot like me. They look—well, *normal*.

"This is one of the few joints we're allowed in outside the Block," he says. "It's not legal per se . . . but the owners here are pretty decent. All the other restaurants and stores have checkpoint scanners when you enter to keep out the mystics."

"Even the drained ones?"

He nods.

"Is that why you brought me here?"

"Sure. Also, I like the coffee."

I look around. Java River's customers seem to come from every walk of life: there are girls and boys my own age who don't seem evil in the least. A group of sandy-haired young men in the window are laughing and playing cards. And at the far end of the long room are a half-dozen oldsters, sipping coffee and watching TV and arguing with each other about what they see there.

Yes, their complexions are wan; their skin is paper-thin. They look weak, fundamentally tired as a result of the drainings. But these people aren't the menacing individuals I've been warned about my entire life—the deviants and drained mystics who supposedly line every street in the Magnificent Block. That is what we were taught at Florence Academy. What I was taught by my parents.

It doesn't seem fair—if they're drained, why can't they go anywhere they want?

The boy seems to be reading my mind. "Not what you expected?"

"No, not exactly."

The waitress comes with our coffee and sets the mugs down in front of us. The boy immediately takes a sip, but I stir mine with a spoon, waiting for it to cool.

We sit like this for a few minutes. I should be going. It's late, and I still need to find Thomas. And yet, something about this mystic is compelling me to stay here.

I clear my throat. "Thank you for saving me. And for . . . my arm."

The unspoken words are: for using your power to heal me.

I don't say them out loud, for fear of who might be listening. Rebel mystics are illegal. These are the people my father hunts down on a daily basis. If he knew I was in the Depths, sitting directly across from a fully empowered mystic . . .

"You're welcome."

He leans forward. His irises are speckled with lighter shades of blue around the edges. He sips his coffee.

"My name is Aria," I say to break the silence.

"Like from an opera." His voice is so soft I can barely hear it.

"Well, yes, actually. My mother's a big fan."

"Any one in particular?"

I squint. "Why, do you know opera?"

"You assume I don't?"

"Well, it's just that—"

"I'm a mystic, so obviously it's impossible for me to have even an *ounce* of culture." His voice is tired, tinged with bitterness. "What do they teach you up there?" He points at the ceiling, but I know he means the Aeries.

"Listen, that was rude of me. I'm sure you're cultured, of course you are. I've just had a bad couple of weeks, and now a really strange night. I'm sorry." I take a big gulp of coffee. "So, um, which is your favorite?"

He stares right at me, and I can see him soften a little. Then the right corner of his mouth twitches just a little, and he breaks into an enormous grin. "I was just teasing you, mostly. I hate opera." He puts his hand over his heart. "I've got more of a rocker's soul."

He laughs as though he's really enjoying himself, and his entire face lights up. I start laughing, too—in fact, I can't stop. It feels so *good*. I can't remember the last time I laughed like this.

"A rocker, huh?" I repeat with a bit of an eye roll, but he knows he's got me. I can see it in his eyes. "So . . . what do you play?"

He gives a quick nod. "Guitar."

"I love music," I say, trying to focus on anything—the floor, the table, my coffee—except how he smells, like smoke and sweat and salt from the canals. "My parents gave me tons of lessons when I was a kid—piano, flute, oboe—but I was never any good."

The mystic raises an eyebrow and looks amused. "I find that hard to believe."

"Oh?"

He looks me up and down, and I feel practically naked; the intensity of his gaze is so strong I can actually feel my stomach churn.

"I'd imagine you're the kind of girl who is good at everything you do."

I know he means it as a compliment, but it makes me think of the overdose. Of failing so completely. Losing my memories to Stic and disappointing my family and Thomas. The scene with Gretchen at the plummet party and the upcoming election.

I shake my head. "Not everything."

"Don't worry about it. I'm bad at tons of things." He offers me a smile while tracing the edge of his coffee mug with a fingertip. It's strange to see his fingers looking so normal when I know what they can do.

"Like what?"

"School," he says. "I was never good at math. Or science. Or anything, really. That's why I dropped out."

I gasp instinctively. "You dropped out of school?"

He chuckles. "There are more important things, you know. At least to some people."

"I suppose," I say tentatively. "So what's important to you, then?"

The boy looks thoughtful for a moment. "Friends. Family."

"That's good," I say, then immediately wonder why it matters to me that we share the same values. It's not like I'll ever see him again.

"And equality," he says, then picks up his mug and takes a long sip. I wonder if that was supposed to be a stab at me. Surely he knows who I am, who my parents are? There's no way a rebel mystic—or anyone from the Depths—could possibly support the Roses and the Fosters. We've been despised by mystics in the Depths for ages—not that we ever really minded, as long as things stayed the same.

I avert my eyes. He must find me despicable, with my wealth and good fortune. Which is disappointing because . . . because why? I glance back at him and I can hear my own heartbeat. Deep down, I know why. I just don't want to admit it.

I like him.

My throat feels dry and scratchy. I'm engaged. I can't like him. I don't even know his name. Thomas's face flashes before me: the richness of his eyes, the honey color of his skin. What am I doing here?

"Aria?"

I look up. "Yeah?"

"Are you okay?"

No! I want to yell, but it's not his fault this conversation is the most comfortable one I've had in ages, that simply looking at him relaxes me. "Are you going to tell me your name?"

He scratches his head, confused, as though he'd been expecting a much more intense question. "Sure. It's Hunter."

I expect him to say more, but he doesn't. "So . . . what else do I need to know about you? We're practically strangers."

Something about the question strikes a chord in him. The muscles around his mouth tense; his posture becomes rigid. The boy I've been talking to suddenly morphs into something harder, colder. He takes out his wallet, removing a few bills and placing them on the table. "No offense," Hunter says, "but it's best if things remain that way."

Then he takes out his phone and punches a few buttons, texting someone.

"Seriously?" I'm confused by the sudden change in tone—one moment we're laughing, the next he's distant, leaving? "I was just attacked. You saved my life. We don't have to be friends or anything, but you don't have to be so . . . so . . ."

"Rude?" He looks up, the pure blue of his eyes still startling. "Look, Aria. You seem like a nice girl, but as long as you're safe, my work is done. My friend Turk is coming to pick you up and take you home. Wait for him here." He narrows his eyes. "Don't come back here, okay? You're safer in the Aeries. Where your sort belongs."

He stands. Simply looking at him makes my heart beat faster. I want him to stay, but there is nothing that ties him to me. We really are strangers. The thought makes my insides ache.

"Goodbye, Aria," he says, and though he's determined, I can tell he's pained.

I sit still, frozen with sadness. Even though he's telling me goodbye, the way he says my name feels like the warmest hello I've ever received.

It's only as he's leaving that I see a tiny tattoo in the center of his left wrist.

In the shape of a starburst.

"Wait!" I slide out of the booth too quickly and fall onto the floor—and now everyone is looking right at me.

"Miss?" someone asks. "Are you okay?"

I get up, shake myself off, and hurry outside. I look around frantically but the streets are practically empty. How did I let him go *again*?

I try to calm my breathing. I wasn't hallucinating—there *was* a boy on my balcony last night, and it wasn't someone who'd been invited to the party.

It was Hunter. He's saved me twice in two nights.

I stand for a few moments underneath the JAVA RIVER awning, hoping he'll return. Then I feel silly for waiting. I'm Aria Rose. I live in the Aeries, and I'm engaged.

Thomas. He's the one I'm supposed to see tonight, and I haven't thought of him once since I saw Hunter.

When I realize Hunter's not returning, I go back inside—my table hasn't been cleared. Behind the cash register, an old woman with grayish skin harrumphs at me, her hair knotted into a bird's nest on top of her head. I sit down to wait for Turk.

Why did Hunter save me in the first place if he didn't want anything to do with me? Without thinking, I stare into my coffee mug and down the scalding liquid in one gulp. I wince. My throat, and my heart, are on fire.

· V ·

With a name like Turk, I'm not sure what to expect. This is what I get:

A boy with copper skin and egg-shaped eyes, hair fashioned into a Mohawk, the sides sheared close to his scalp, the top ablaze with color, morphing from black at the roots to bright platinum near the tips. Silver piercings run through his earlobes and his right eyebrow. His clothes are tight and black, long pants and a sleeveless shirt exposing hills and heaps of muscle. His arms are colored from wrist to armpit with tattoos: fire-breathing dragons and dangerous-looking swords, nearly naked women and strange mythological creatures.

He has the same healthy coloring as Hunter—another rebel. His legs straddle a white motorcycle with chrome wheels and black accents on the seat. I've only seen a motorcycle on the Internet and never would have guessed how *big* they are. He spots me through the window and beckons me outside.

On the street, the hot summer air makes me feel like I'm in a sauna. Turk holds out a sleek silver helmet and cocks his head. "You gonna get on?"

He must be kidding. "Absolutely not."

"So you're just gonna hang out here?"

Good point. I have to get back to the Aeries, and I can't afford a gondola—the rest of my money was hidden in my cloak.

Turk extends the helmet a second time. "You seem like a reasonable girl, Aria. Let me get you home in one piece. I'd say you're a bit out of your league."

"How does this thing work?" I ask skeptically, eyeing the cycle. The engine is nearly twice the size of my head, the exhaust pipes polished to a shine. "It looks too big for most of the streets."

Turk laughs. "Let's just say this sucker is . . . enhanced." He winks. "For your riding pleasure."

"Okay," I say, grabbing the helmet and slipping it on. I go to climb on the cycle but there's only one seat—and he's on it.

Turk slaps one of his thighs. "Step on up, sweetheart."

I raise my eyebrows. Turk matches my expression.

I groan. "Don't do anything funny."

"Nope," Turk says, offering me his hand. "Nothing funny about this at all."

He hoists me up and I settle between his legs. He presses a button and a sleek pair of handlebars extend from a slot in the front of the bike.

Turk leans forward, his arms wrapping around me when he grabs the bars. "Ready?" he asks, lips close to my ear, his breath warm and sweet.

"Sure," I say.

"Just tell me where to go," he says.

I whisper my directions as Turk pushes a tiny button and we erupt in flames.

Turk's bike really *is* enhanced. Magical, even.

We tip forward on the narrow streets, so drastically I have no idea how gravity is functioning, so fast there's no time to be sick, veering left, then right, skipping over broken concrete and garbage and shattered bottles, building after building bleeding into each other as we pass.

We whirl and zoom past a fleet of gondolas tied up for the night, sleeping in the black water, their prows knotted to posts along the sidewalks. The cycle is narrow enough to creep over a stone bridge, nimble enough to take hairpin turns in alleyways.

Our only exchange is the way our bodies move with the bike, how Turk's arms are snug around me. I close my eyes and imagine he is someone else.

And then we stop.

The handlebars retract and Turk leaps off the motorcycle, landing with both feet firmly on the ground. I slide less gracefully off the side and remove my helmet—my hair is wet, matted to my forehead. I scrape my fingers through it as Turk watches me.

"What?" I say.

"Nothing. Nice to meet you, Aria."

He's about to remount when I stop him. "Wait," I say, my hand on his arm. "I need to ask you something."

"About?"

"Hunter." He smiles knowingly, and the look on his face tells me he's been expecting this. "I know you two are friends," I say, "and . . ."

"You don't know anything about him?"

"Exactly."

"There's not much to know."

"What's that supposed to mean?"

Turk shrugs. "Hunter's a mysterious guy. If he wants to tell you something, he'll tell you. If he doesn't, he won't." Turk cradles the helmet he lent me under one of his arms. "But do yourself a favor. Just let things be. Forget about him."

Forget. Something I am quite good at, apparently.

"Well, I appreciate the ride, at least," I say softly.

"The pleasure was all mine," Turk says. He straddles the motorcycle, places the helmet in his lap so he can use both hands, and starts the engine. "Be careful. You know what you're doing?"

I glance at the POD a few steps away. His question makes it clear that he knows I gave him directions to Thomas's apartment building and not my own. Granted, we live on opposite sides of the city, so it wouldn't take a brain surgeon to figure out I'm heading in the wrong direction. But at least Turk isn't trying to stop me from going.

"I'm fine. Thanks." I point to the helmet. "Aren't you going to wear that?" I yell over the roar of the cycle.

Turk only smirks. "Of course not." He points to his Mohawk, which has somehow remained unharmed despite our travels. "I don't want to mess up my hair."

Then he's gone, leaving behind a cloud of fast-fading sparks.

Thomas is surprised to see me. Which kind of figures, since it *is* around midnight.

"Aria?" He shoots an irritated glance at the manservant who ushered me in.

"They announced Ms. Rose on the intercom, sir. I assumed you had arranged to meet her." He reminds me of my father's man, Bartholomew—same white hair, same bland features.

"I did no such thing, Devlin," Thomas says. His hair is messy tonight, without any gel. I like it more this way. "You should know better."

"I'm sorry, sir," Devlin says, bowing his head.

Thomas is far from properly dressed—he's wearing a pair of linen pajama pants. His shirt is unbuttoned, and he hides his chest by crossing his arms. It's not the kind of chest that should be hidden: broad shoulders and sculpted pectorals lightly dusted with hair. His stomach is tight and flat. Thomas is more muscular than I imagined, more athletic.

I must be staring, because he reaches over, lifting my chin with his fingers so I'm looking at his face instead of his abdomen.

"What are you doing here, Aria?" He sounds almost unhappy.

"I—I wanted to see you." Which is partly true, but not for the reasons I'm implying. I'm thankful for the cool air in his apartment after being outside in the deadly heat, but my pants and shirt are wet with sweat, and now I'm beginning to shiver.

Thomas purses his lips. "Do your parents know you're here?"

"Of course not." I reach out and touch his bicep. "Why does it matter? We didn't care about them before, did we?" My voice has gotten louder, but I can't help it. "We need to talk, Thomas." I look at Devlin. "Alone. It's important."

Thomas is silent, his face unreadable. Then Devlin says, "Shall I frisk her, sir?"

I step back. "You're kidding, right? Why would I carry anything dangerous?"

"Not harm me," Thomas says. "Harm *you*."

It takes a second, but then I get it. He's worried I have Stic on me.

I'm left with no choice. Devlin pats me down, pressing his hands against my arms and torso and legs. Then he runs a handheld scanner over every inch of my body. Its insistent beeping makes me want to smack someone. I've never felt so humiliated in my life. Thomas doesn't even have the decency to frisk me himself.

Finally, Devlin announces, "Clean."

"I could have told you that," I say with a snarl.

"It's protocol, Aria. Not personal," Thomas says. "Devlin, please take Aria to my bedroom. I'll be there momentarily." He turns to me. "My parents are at a charity function. I need to call them and check when they'll be home so they won't find you here. I don't want you to get into any trouble."

Devlin bows a second time and motions down the hallway. "Please, miss, follow me." Once we are far enough away, he whispers, "Sorry about the scanner, miss."

The Fosters' home is sleeker than ours: simple, clean lines, modern-looking furniture. There is no carpet anywhere; no hardwood floors, either. Instead, each room is tiled in shiny colors. For the first time in my life, I miss my mother's antique end tables, tubular vases, and thick drapes.

Mystic paintings in sleek black frames are spaced throughout the apartment; the colors swirl together as though the paint is alive, moving just enough so that the images never stay exactly the same for more than a few seconds.

I stop for a moment and study one—an oil painting of the city skyline—and watch as the sky darkens from gray to blue to black, then back to gray again. It's stunning, really.

I could stare for hours, but I move on.

Thomas's room is nearly bare—a large bed on a black platform against the far wall. A desk with his TouchMe and a chair that looks more impressive than comfortable. Two framed movie posters—Charlie Chaplin's *A King in New York* and *Cat on a Hot Tin Roof* with Paul Newman—and three long windows overlooking the East Side skyline. The walls are white; the floor is black. A gray lamp with a metal body sits on a nightstand.

Devlin leaves me alone in the room. After a minute or two, I start to snoop.

I press the touchpad next to his closet and sift through his clothes—dozens of pants and shirts and suits and ties, unadventurous in terms of color and style. More appropriate for men our fathers' age than for a seventeen-year-old who just graduated from prep school.

Then to his bathroom, where I search through the cabinets. Nothing odd to report, except for a bottle of mystic headache reliever like the one Kiki carries with her. I leave the bathroom and glance at his nightstand: an aMuseMe and a pair of headphones, and a glass of water. Thomas is neat. Clean. Seems to be hiding nothing.

I'm not sure what I'm looking for exactly—my room has been wiped clean, but surely there must be some proof of our love that he's held on to.

Then I hear hushed voices approaching. Devlin and Thomas. I face the doorway, trying my best to look innocent.

Thomas steps inside and presses a panel on the wall; the door closes with Devlin still outside. Thomas wordlessly slips on a checkered flannel bathrobe from his closet, wrapping the ties around his waist. He hasn't shaved today, and he seems tougher than he did at the party last night. More natural. More dangerous.

I wait for him to continue scolding me. Instead, he sighs and collapses on his bed. He pats the empty spot next to him. "Hi," he says softly.

"Hi," I say back, sitting next to him.

"I'm sorry about before. You just caught me off guard."

"I don't deserve to be treated like that, Thomas. I didn't do anything wrong."

He puffs out a breath. "Oh no? You only took Stic without telling me."

"I'm sorry," I say. "Honestly. I don't remember *why* I did it, but there must have been a reason. But that's not me. You know it's not . . . don't you?"

He scooches closer. "Maybe you were upset about something. I'm just sorry you didn't feel like you could share that with me. I need to be a part of your life, Aria. We're going to be married. We can't keep secrets from each other." He pulls me to him. It feels awkward.

"Are you friends with Gretchen Monasty?"

I can feel Thomas's body tense. "Why?"

"I saw her today," I say, "at a plummet. And she mentioned you, and . . . well, she said that you spoke to her about me, and I'm just wondering what you said. Did you tell her about the overdose?"

Thomas looks offended. "I would never. My parents and I agreed to keep that private, for everyone's sake."

"Would you have said anything else?"

"Absolutely not," Thomas says. "I barely know the girl."

I think back to this afternoon, to what Gretchen suggested. Why would she lie? Then I look at Thomas. Why would *he*?

"Were you anywhere near my clutch? The bag I carried last night?"

Thomas widens his eyes, pressing his hand to my shoulder. "Aria, are you okay?"

"I think so," I say. I can tell he's wary of me now, suspicious of my mental health. I need a different tactic.

I reach for his chest, where his heart is, and feel its steady beat. His breathing is jagged, short. His eyes are wide open.

"Touch me," I say suddenly.

He coughs. "What?"

"Touch my heart."

His right hand moves slowly, as though it's been dipped in molasses, fingers spread so that I can see the spaces between them. Ever so lightly, he presses just underneath my collarbone.

"Lower," I tell him, loosing my shirt and moving his hand inside. His fingers edge over the top of my breast. We both tremble, and I am sure: we have never done anything like this before.

"There," I say. "Can you feel that? My heartbeat?"

He gulps, staring at me. "Yes."

"Tell me a story," I say, closing my eyes again.

"What do you mean?" Thomas asks.

"Tell me about us. Something romantic. Please." Even if I can't remember our relationship, maybe for my parents' sake, for Thomas's sake, and for the love of the Aeries, I can learn to love him.

I try to picture Thomas in my mind, in my memory. His hand is deliciously hot against my body, and mine against his. His chest rises and falls beneath my touch.

Eventually, he speaks:

"Right. Let me see. The first time we ever kissed was in a gondola, at night. Not night, exactly—nearly night. Dusk. You were wearing, um, a short red dress that showed off your legs. We met at our usual place near the Magnificent Block, and then we took a gondola around the city. I stepped in first to help you, but the boat was rocking, and you almost fell right into the water. I caught you, though, and you sort of . . . melted right into me. I leaned down and kissed you. It was like how it is in the movies—sort of slow at first, but wonderful. We were both a little sweaty, and the gondolier was giving us weird looks, but we just laughed at him. We didn't care. We were just happy to be together. I never wanted to stop kissing you, Aria. Never."

I'm about to tell him that I don't remember this when a memory pops into my brain and I go silent. Images from his story begin to color the blackness in my head until the moment comes alive: I am waiting underneath a building with a broken awning near the Block. I remember running to meet someone—Thomas?—and falling into the gondola, just like he said.

The images unfold out of nowhere, but they are so vivid it's like I'm seeing them in Technicolor. It's dazzling. Then my memory of Thomas goes blurry. His features go liquid and rearrange themselves, his nose lengthening, eyes broadening and tightening, lips stretching into a scary grin. When he moves, there is a delay, the rest of his body microseconds behind his head.

I shake my head hard, and everything fizzles out.

Gray.

White.

My mind is a blur, and then it is blank.

I open my eyes and I am back in Thomas's room, on his bed. We are still touching, only his hand feels heavy now. My palm is sweaty and I lift it from his chest. "Weird."

"What's wrong?" he asks, looking concerned. "Are you okay?"

"Not really," I say. "Something just happened to me. Something—"

The sound of shattering glass interrupts me. There in the door are my parents, standing with shocked expressions on their faces. My father is in a dark suit, his dress shirt open at the neck, the knot of his yellow and blue tie loosened. A water glass is in pieces on the floor. I must have knocked it over.

"Aria, you're leaving. Now," my father says, letting out a growl.

Thomas sits up and distances himself from me on the bed.

I turn back to Thomas. "You called my *parents*?"

In a flash, my father is there beside the bed, grabbing my shoulder. His fingers dig into my flesh; I yelp, then stifle my scream. There is no use in fighting—I've been caught. I glare at Thomas, boring a hole into him with my eyes.

I feel incredibly betrayed.

My father drags me down the hallway and out of the apartment.

I don't question it when we descend into the Depths instead of taking the light-rail across the Aeries. Stiggson and Klartino, two of my father's men, walk behind me; I follow my parents down a tiny, trash-strewn street to a broad canal—Lexington Avenue— lined with docks where gondoliers wait for fares. They glance at us, curious, clearly struck by the oddity of our presence.

My father finally speaks to me. "Did one of them take you across?"

I study the men. "No." I'm not sure why he's asking. It can't be for a good reason.

We walk along the canal. Spot another group of gondoliers. None of them looks familiar.

"Johnny, what is the point of this?" my mother asks.

"Be quiet." He turns to me, lips pulled back into a snarl. "Any of these men?"

I shake my head.

We travel across a handful of streets, closer and closer to the Magnificent Block, stopping whenever we see gondoliers. Sweat drips from every part of me; the night is sweltering. My shoes pinch my toes. All I want is to go home.

Finally, we come across a lone gondolier waiting near the side of the canal. My father stops, Klartino and Stiggson at either side. "Is this him?"

I study the man. His hair is dirty and his cheeks are speckled with pockmarks. It is not the red-haired boy whose gondola I rode in, but he might as well get the dressing-down my father intends to give the boy. It won't matter one way or another to a gondolier, and my father's anger will only worsen the longer we keep walking.

"Sure," I say, exhausted.

The gondolier looks bewildered. "Sir, what do you want? I don't got no money."

My father laughs, happy for the first time all evening. Klartino and Stiggson follow with menacing chuckles. Dad looks at me and says, "Listen to me and listen carefully, Aria. I don't know what you were playing at tonight, but the fun is over. You are not to do anything to jeopardize this marriage. *Anything.* Do you hear me?"

His voice is grating and scary, his face full of anger.

"Yes," I manage to get out. "I hear you. I'm sorry."

Dad's body relaxes at my apology. "Good girl," he says. "That's settled, then."

I sigh in relief.

"Oh, and Aria?" my father says. His thick eyebrows are raised, the lines of his forehead thin and dark.

"Yes?"

He reaches into his waistband, removes a silver pistol, and—before I have time to blink—shoots the gondolier in the head. It's deafeningly loud. I exhale a sharp cry.

The man crumples like a puppet and tumbles backward,

splashing into the canal and floating on the water. Without being directed, my father's bodyguards pick up an oar and drag the man in. They'll dispose of his body later, I know.

My father hands the gun to one of his men, dusts off his hands, and calmly says to me, "Never sneak out of the apartment again."

· VI ·

When they've finished filling six vials with my blood, it's time to move to another room.

"Come with me," says one of the nurses, a blimplike woman in a tight white coat, her wheat-colored hair pulled back into a severe ponytail.

I follow her into a larger room with an enormous rectangular machine. Everything is white and sterile. I feel dirty in comparison. I am in a teal hospital gown tied loosely in the back. My feet are bare.

It is the day after I watched my father kill a man, and we have still not spoken. My mother refuses to discuss it, and my father went straight to bed when we arrived home last night. He was already gone when I woke up this morning.

"The doctor will be ready in a moment," the nurse says, closing the door behind her, leaving me alone.

With my thoughts.

I have always known that my father is dangerous. You don't get to be the head of a family that controls half of Manhattan without spilling a little blood. But until now, he has always been careful to keep me as ignorant as possible of his dirty deeds. Every time I close my eyes, I see that gondolier tumble backward. That poor man! He'd done nothing wrong, but he lost his life because I was tired and sweaty, because I said he'd done something he didn't do.

I keep seeing the man's face over and over in my head. I am responsible, and it feels horrible. I know my father is capable of killing again, and I refuse to be the cause. From now on I'll do anything to keep him from hurting others—even if it means submitting to his will.

"Good to see you, Aria."

I look up. Dr. May has entered the room. He walks past me, the nurse trailing behind him like a pet dog. My mother is just inside the door, watching anxiously.

Dr. May opens a drawer filled with latex gloves and pulls on a pair. Then he removes a pair of wire-rimmed glasses from the pocket of his lab coat. Glasses are rare these days—most people have surgery to correct their vision as early as possible. But he is old-fashioned and, well, old. Like the examination room, everything about him is white: the thin strands of hair that sit atop his head, the chalky pallor of his skin, his mustache and, of course, his clothes.

"Aria," he says. "How do you feel?"

There are so many ways I could answer that question. "Okay."

Dr. May snaps his fingers and the nurse darts up to him with a folder, avoiding eye contact. "Your mother tells me you are still suffering from minor memory loss."

"It's not minor." The hospital gown is stiff against my skin. "It's very serious," I say, wondering if Dr. May can erase the image of my father's face as he pulled the trigger. I shake my head and steel my nerves.

"Indeed. The brain works in mysterious ways. But there are some things that can help make it less mysterious." He motions to the massive machine at the far end of the room. It's long and thin, like a coffin, with one open end. A long silver table extends from it, and he motions for me to lie down. I do, and he prepares a syringe, clear liquid spurting out the needle tip as he tests it.

Behind him is an entire wall of medical instruments, displayed like trophies: scalpels of varying lengths; syringes, some as thick as my wrist, others so thin as to nearly be invisible. There are instruments I could not even begin to name, metal curves and hooks and things that grip and expand, contract, sew—a terrifying collection.

"What's the needle for?" I ask.

"Relax," Dr. May says, taking my arm. His glove feels powdery against my skin. "So many questions."

"I can't ask questions?"

He looks at me and laughs. At least, I think he laughs—the sound is forced and screechy. Unnatural. "Of course you can," he says. "I just don't have to answer them."

Then he jabs the needle into one of the veins inside my elbow.

When he is done, Dr. May discards the needle, smooths his mustache with two fingers, and scribbles notes in a thick manila file.

After, he swiftly prepares another needle, this time with a blue liquid, and pricks me again. Then another. And another. They grow increasingly painful.

"These injections will help speed your recovery," the doctor says. "Now, Aria, we're going to slide you in here to get some clear pictures of your brain. We did this after your overdose, but now that your system has had time to clear the Stic from your body, perhaps we'll get different results. How does that sound?"

"Okay." Maybe the test will explain what's going on inside my head. "Oh, and Doctor?"

"Yes?" he asks.

"Yesterday, I think I felt a memory of Thomas returning . . . but it was strange."

"Strange how?"

I look at him to gauge his reaction. "I was remembering something Thomas and I did together, but all the parts of the memory—the way he looked, the sounds, the smells—were just . . . off. Like they'd happened to someone else. Or were part of a bad video."

Dr. May looks puzzled. He exchanges a quick glance with my mother. "I'm glad you told me." His nervousness bothers me. If he truly wanted my memory to come back, he would be excited that I remembered Thomas. Wouldn't he? Instead, he looks . . . worried. Frightened, even.

The question is, *why?*

Then he goes back to his table and prepares one more shot. It takes him a moment to find a place to jab me; my entire right arm is beginning to bruise.

After the injection, Dr. May hands the nurse the empty syringe. "Now, Patricia here will operate the machine. Once you're done, she'll escort you to my office, where we can discuss the next steps in your recovery. Just lie back, Aria, and relax."

Relax. As if it were that easy.

There is a whirring at first once I'm slid inside, then a rhythmic banging, like someone is taking a hammer to the side of the machine.

Bang bang bang. Dr. May exchanging glances with my mother. *Bang bang bang.* My father shoots a man in the head. *Bang bang bang.* Thomas, his heart beneath my hand. *Bang bang bang.* I am getting sleepy. *Bang bang bang.* Turk's motorcycle. *Bang bang bang.* Hunter's touch healing the gash in my arm. *Bang bang bang.* What is wrong with me? What has happened to my life? Will I ever have any control?

Bang bang bang.
Bang bang bang.
Bang bang bang.

"That wasn't too bad, was it?" Patricia asks once she wheels me out of the machine and I can see the light again. I am still for a moment; then I swing my legs over the side of the table.

I grunt. What does *she* know about bad. "How long was I asleep for?"

She looks at the clock on the wall. "About three hours."

I shake my head. Three hours?

"Don't worry," she says, "it's a long procedure."

What could they possibly have done to me that took three hours? The whole thing feels wrong, but I know fighting my father and anyone on his payroll right now is dangerous. I feel so alone. I watch as Patricia shuts down the machine.

"Come on," she says, motioning for me to follow. "I'll bring you to the doctor."

We stroll down a long corridor, passing another examination room every few feet. I stare at the white carpet as we walk.

Dr. May's office has a rectangular plaque—

DR. SALVADOR MAY

—on the door. Patricia points, then starts back down the corridor. I knock softly, but there's no response. So I press my ear to the opaque glass; surprisingly, I can hear voices on the other side. I brace my hand against the wall and listen.

"Really, Melinda, I wouldn't be so worried—"

"How can you say that," my mother says, "when the last time was such a failure?"

"This time will be different," Dr. May says, "this time will be—"

Suddenly, the door retracts and I fall into the office. I must have pressed a touchpad accidentally. I land with my hands and knees on the carpeted floor. Then I pick myself up and brush off the hospital gown.

Dr. May and my mother stare at me like I'm deranged. I shrug and say, "Sorry."

"Aria!" my mother says, her face aghast. "Haven't you heard of knocking? It's not as though you were raised by a pack of wolves."

"Please, sit down." Dr. May motions to an empty chair. His

desk is cluttered with family photographs and a stack of files that teeters dangerously near the edge.

"The results of the exam are uploaded instantly into my TouchMe," he says, scrolling the screen with his finger. "And from what I can tell, you have a beautiful brain." He smiles without showing his teeth. I think it's an attempt to be comforting.

What am I supposed to say to that? "Great. Beautiful brain," I repeat.

"I'm confident that your amnesia will fade in time," Dr. May continues. "The effects of Stic are still not completely understood, as the energy from every mystic is as unique as a fingerprint. Did you know that mystics have different-colored hearts?"

I did, but only now do I imagine the oddness of, say, a yellow heart. But aren't we all just a multitude of colors inside—red arteries and blue veins and pink muscle? Perhaps a yellow heart isn't so odd after all.

"Stic is nothing more than distilled mystic energy. Depending on who it comes from, the effects will vary," says Dr. May. "It's impossible for us to know exactly what you ingested. Luckily, there seems to have been no lasting damage." He shuts off the screen and folds his hands on top of his desk. I stare at him and rub the inside of my arm, which aches from the shots. "I know it's been difficult for you, Aria, but I *am* hopeful that you will be feeling better in no time. The injections today will help."

"Thank you, Dr. May," my mother says, seeming satisfied. I'm not convinced, though.

Suddenly, I hold out my open palm, hoping she'll find it with hers. Even though she hasn't held my hand in years. Even though we are not close like that.

Instead, she stands and kisses Dr. May softly on the cheek, careful not to leave behind any trace of her lipstick. "That is quite a relief," she says. "Isn't it, Aria?"

I close my waiting fingers into a fist, nod, and say, "Yes. *Quite.*"

That evening, I search my closet for the perfect dress. I've never thought much about all the clothes I own, but after yesterday, I can't stop thinking about the Depths and how, in comparison, everything in my apartment is so . . . expensive.

I select a peach-colored minidress with a high waist and beaded fringe around the hem. Why does my family have so much money? It's never made much sense to me—my mother doesn't work, and sure, my father collects bribes from city officials, but that can't account for the insane amount of wealth the Roses have amassed over the years. Can it? I don't think I've ever bothered to ask about any of the details.

I glance in the mirror and fix my hair. I'm being forced to go on a date with Thomas. And a chaperone. It seems that despite the fact that Thomas called my parents and let his servant frisk me last night, and despite the mind-numbing guilt I feel over the man my father shot, I'm expected to be seen with my fiancé for the sake of the election. Expected to be happy. The best I can hope for is that last night was a fluke. That Thomas was, as he said, caught off guard by my visit and wasn't acting like himself. That we can still fall in love. Again.

I feel like my body has been taken over by puppeteers. I'm so tired, and even as I dress, I feel the strings above my head being pulled—by Dr. May, by my mother and father, by Thomas. No one gets close enough to touch me; they maneuver me from above.

"Make sure to smile," my mother says as I'm about to leave the apartment with Klartino. "You never know when someone is going to take your picture, Aria."

"I will." I clench my teeth and smile so widely that my face hurts. My mother rolls her eyes and walks away, down the hall that leads to my father's study. I haven't had a bodyguard in over a year, and Klartino isn't exactly my first choice for a chaperone. He has thick, nubby hands and a sour-looking face; the entire right side of his neck is covered in a green-ink tattoo of a tiger clenching a rose in its teeth. Nice.

But I guess after the stunt I pulled last night, I'm not exactly my parents' favorite person at the moment. And Klartino *is* pretty intimidating. I wonder how he and Stiggson disposed of the gondolier's body. If he cared at all that a man died right in front of him.

Probably not.

We're eating at the Purple Pussycat, a throwback to the speak-easies of the 1920s. The restaurant is owned by Thomas's family and sits atop a spiral building on Fifth Avenue. The décor is all high ceilings and walls paneled with dark mahogany, shiny black floors, and various bars set into pockets of the room. Men and women sip fancy drinks, the men in smart suits with crisp shirts and ties, the women in tailored dresses that expose their arms and legs, pointy shoes that surely crush their toes.

Klartino stays a few paces behind me as I approach the hostess, a girl in her early twenties with the Foster five-point star tattooed on the inside of her left wrist. She shows me to a table where Thomas is already seated.

Thomas stands as I approach. He looks smart in a white dress shirt and dark slacks, the outfit completed by a paisley tie and navy-blue blazer. His hair is more like it was at the engagement party than at his apartment—gelled and parted on the side. I see flashes of light—paparazzi—and I realize this is a carefully orchestrated photo op. We're the ideal couple—groomed to perfection, encouraging people in the Depths to vote for Garland Foster in the election instead of the mystic candidate Violet Brooks.

Diners bow their heads and whisper about the soon-to-be-married couple with the potential to unite the East and West sides of Manhattan against the mystic threat.

I smile—like my mother instructed—to hide how sour that makes me feel.

Now more than ever, I feel a lot of weight on my (bare) shoulders.

"Aria, you look beautiful," Thomas says, kissing my cheek. I close my eyes, wondering how strong I will have to be to endure this "till death do us part."

"For a Rose, anything," I whisper, repeating my grandmother's old adage of familial devotion.

"Hmmm?" Thomas says.

Suddenly, something stirs within me—a memory, an emotion, I'm not sure. It's almost as if a voice in my head is whispering,

You love Thomas Foster. Even though I don't *feel* the truth of it in my bones, if it weren't true, why would I be thinking it? My mind and my body feel completely out of sync.

The shots this morning, the machine . . . maybe they *did* work, and my memories are coming back. I glance again at Thomas—I'm so confused that I wind up curtseying and holding on to the ends of my dress too long, imprinting my palms with marks from the beaded fringe. "No, *you* look beautiful!" I say, and from out of nowhere I get the hiccups.

"Aria?" Thomas says.

"I'm fine," I say. "Really"—*hic!*—"I am."

Klartino offers me a sip of water, and I take it. "Thank"—*hic!*—"you."

Thomas reaches for my shoulder, which startles me—a good thing, actually, because I stop hiccupping. His hand is warm on my skin. I can't deny his sex appeal, how smooth and polished he is. Would marrying him be the worst thing in the world? By now, the entire restaurant is staring; dozens of eyes have zoomed in on me, and a handful of cameras are snapping my picture.

"We should sit down," I say.

Thomas nods. "Good idea."

I wave Klartino close; he hunches his already hunched back and brings his ear to my lips. "You're free to go," I whisper.

He shakes his head. "Your father said I'm supposed to stay with you."

"Can you at least sit at another table?" I pull in my chair and place the napkin on my lap. If my relationship with Thomas has to be watched, it can be watched from a distance.

Klartino calls over the hostess, who seats him at a table in direct sight of ours. "The food better be good," he mutters.

When I turn my attention back to Thomas, he's scrolling through the menu.

"See anything you like?" I ask.

He glances at me and lets out a low whistle. "I certainly do."

Thomas's stare lingers for a few seconds, as though there is something about my face that he finds particularly appealing. I shiver even though I'm not cold. A gorgeous boy—a boy I'm about to *marry*—is complimenting me, coming on to me. I can live with that, right? I'm a Rose. I can make sacrifices for power.

So why does Hunter's face pop into my head?

Thomas orders dinner for us, but I can't seem to focus on what he's telling the waiter. Instead, I hear the strange voice again: *You love Thomas Foster.* It's distant, as though it exists wholly outside my body. I close my eyes, imagining I'm looking down at myself, watching a girl in love with her fiancé.

"Why did you call my parents last night?"

Thomas looks up from his glass, startled. "What?"

"My parents. Last night. You called them—why? Did you want to get me in trouble?"

He shakes his head. "Of course not. Devlin called them, not me. I had no idea what he'd done until they showed up."

I stare at him, his perfectly chiseled features, and wonder if he's telling the truth. If anything, he looks concerned. Upset, even. "Okay," I say. "I believe you." Thomas lets out a deep breath; he seems relieved. "How was your day?" I ask. It's what my mom always asks my dad.

Thomas relaxes into his chair. "Good. My day was good."

"What did you do?"

"I trailed Garland on a few meetings," he says offhandedly. "The mayor wants to raise the number of drainings per mystic from two to four per year, and he wanted to walk Garland through the process."

"More drainings?"

Thomas shrugs. "Why not?"

"Isn't two enough?"

"I have no idea," Thomas answers. Our first appetizer, bacon-wrapped scallops, is set on the table. "But he must think more drainings will keep them down. The last thing we want is for these mystics to regenerate too quickly and overthrow us all with their weirdo magic. Plus, they're thinking of lowering the required draining age from thirteen to ten."

"Ten? Isn't that a bit young?"

Thomas forks one of the scallops into his mouth. "They say that a mystic's powers mature at thirteen, but what if that's a load of crap? There could be a bunch of crazy-powerful little *freaks* running around. We've gotta end that before it begins, don't you think?"

He says this so casually. I can't help but think of all the people at Java River, most of whom were surely mystics. They already looked beaten down by the officially mandated two drainings per year; how much worse will it be if that's doubled? If the age is lowered? Would it make them sick—or even kill them?

"Maybe they *should* be allowed to keep some of their powers."

Hunter comes to mind, the way he pressed his fingers to my wrist and instantly healed my wound. "Would that really be so bad?"

"Are you serious?" Thomas rests his fork on his plate. "The mystics set off a bomb that wiped out much of Lower Manhattan. Or did you already forget the Conflagration? Their power is *deadly*. They want to *kill* us, Aria. And you're proposing that we let them keep their powers?"

I shake my head. "That's not what I meant."

"What did you mean, then?"

"I meant . . . maybe not *all* mystics want to kill us."

Thomas laughs heartily, right from his belly. "Don't be a fool, Aria. The mystics would love nothing more than to see us all die so they can control the city." He leans forward. "Especially you."

Our waiter clears away the empty appetizer plates and sets down a palate cleanser—an apple and calvados sorbet—before our first course.

"Is it hot in here?" I ask. Thomas shakes his head. "Because I feel . . . hot," I say, using my napkin to dab at my forehead. My skin feels itchy, too—no, not itchy, but . . . tingly, as if somebody were poking at my insides with a live wire.

"Did you know," Thomas says, wiping the corners of his mouth with his napkin, "that mystic workers are actually trying to start some kind of union? Mark Goldlit in the Council saw one of their proposals. They want *vacation*—can you believe it? And Violet Brooks is supporting this nonsense. If we let them get a foothold with the voters, soon all the poor will want a voice in the government, and then what? Too bad mystics can't be stripped of their voting rights like they are their powers. Then we wouldn't even have to worry about the election."

I'm about to say something biting when I stop myself, tasting the sorbet instead and letting it slide down my throat, numbing me. Thomas is just like his brother. Who is just like his father. Who is, for the most part, just like *my* father. To support the mystics would be blasphemy. I trusted Thomas once, enough to fall in love with him. What changed?

Oh, right—I OD'd. An immense wave of guilt washes over me. Thomas's odd behavior is probably because of *me*. Because I messed up and forgot him. Forgot *us*. He probably has no clue how to act around me.

Thomas takes another bite of his sorbet. "It's good, right?"

The more he talks, the more tiny snippets of—what? memory?—pop to life: lips brushing my cheek, a strong hand on my waist. Running. Hiding. The salty smell of water from the Depths.

Is this my past resurfacing? What I used to feel for Thomas, what made me want to risk it all—my parents' affection, my brother's concern, my friends' companionship—to be with him?

Whatever happened at the doctor's office today, whatever was in those shots, is working. When I look at Thomas, every inch of my skin buzzes, from my toes all the way up to my scalp. I want to jump across the table and rip off his tie, lick his neck, kiss his chin, his lips—it's strange, to feel such repulsion at his words and attraction to his body at the same time.

"Aria?" Thomas pushes his water toward me. "Drink this. You look like you're burning up. Are you sick?"

I swallow the water quickly. "No, no. I'm fine." I glance to my left and see an older couple staring; the woman cups her hand over her mouth and whispers something to the man. "I'm just going to use the restroom."

A waiter points to the back of the restaurant, and I move as quickly as I possibly can. Sweat is rolling down my back; my pulse is racing. I can barely walk.

Is this what they call love?

I stand at the sink and splash cool water on my face. What's happening to me? I blot my cheeks with a soft towel the bathroom attendee hands me, then open my clutch.

There, staring back at me, is the locket.

Remember.

I slip it on and wonder what Thomas's reaction will be.

We make our way through the rest of the meal with hardly any conversation.

Fine. "Thomas?" I say finally.

"Mmm?"

"What if we ditched Klartino and went to the Depths? Just you and me?"

Thomas nearly chokes on a piece of meat. "Excuse me?"

"You heard me."

Thomas stares at me curiously. "Are you out of your mind? Why would I go to the Depths?"

Because that's where we escaped together to be happy, I'm about to say, *and maybe we could feel like that again.* But his expression is so cross I can't get the words out.

"Never mind," I say, running my finger under the chain around my neck. "You haven't said a word about my locket."

Thomas eyes where the silvery heart rests against my collarbone. "You shouldn't wear junk like that," he tells me. "It looks like the mystic crap they sell to tourists."

My fiancé turns his attention back to his meal. Slowly, I remove the locket. Thomas didn't give it to me. Who did?

· VII ·

After dinner, Thomas promises Klartino a thousand dollars if he lets us kiss in private.

We three are standing directly outside the light-rail station near the northeast bridge of my building. Klartino nods. "I'll wait for you in the lobby," he says to me. "Don't take too long."

Thomas takes my hand and pulls me out of the light, to the edge of the platform. My back is against the station's glass wall. Beyond that is emptiness. We seem to hover over the city.

This is what I am thinking about—the dark drop to the Depths just on the other side of the glass, the long fall Hunter saved me from—when Thomas kisses me.

I wait to see if I feel anything, for our marriage's sake, but the voice telling me I love him is gone. At least for now. It's just lips touching. No spark.

"Is something wrong?" he asks as I pull away. His hands feel hot—too hot—against my shoulders. I shake free. His brown eyes are open with concern, his mouth smudged with traces of my lipstick. A lock of chocolate-colored hair is curled across his forehead.

"No," I say, wiping his lips clean with my thumb. Pushing back his hair. The nighttime shadows play over his face; he looks even more handsome than he did in the restaurant. "It's just that . . . I should be getting inside. I'm exhausted."

Part of me expects Thomas to insist that I stay outside in the blazing heat with him, to tell me that he can't bear to live a single second without me, even though I suspect that isn't true.

But he only nods and touches two fingers to my forehead. "Go to sleep, Aria. You've had a long day." He pivots and disappears back inside the station.

I slowly cross the platform and step onto the bridge that leads toward my family's apartment. In the distance I see a figure slip out the back entrance of my building, the same entrance I used last night. I recognize the person's cloak immediately—Davida.

What is she doing?

Davida appears to be heading downtown. Even though Klartino is waiting for me in the lobby of my building, I decide to follow her. I'm a few feet behind, on a separate bridge that runs parallel to hers, but I do my best to keep up.

The shadows from the buildings make it difficult to see her as she weaves in and out of the light, from bridge to bridge. My feet are killing me, and the arcs of the bridges make it harder to run than if I were simply on flat pavement. Damn these heels.

I pass four or five apartment buildings, then reach Seventy-Second Street and cross at the intersection, heading east. Davida's stride is relentless, and she increases the distance between us with each step. The only way I'll be able to catch her is to flat-out run.

Just as I am deciding to do that, I am jolted by a blast of yellow-green light and an intense noise: a power station on my left.

Four men are working, their grimy hands occupied with tools. The power station is a prismlike building with iridescent sides, one of the various triangular skyscrapers spaced around the city to give energy to the power grid. A hatch is open and a tangle of tubes is exposed—thick, snaking glass piping full of bright green mystic energy. The energy pulses and swirls like it's alive.

One of the men, with sandy-colored hair and a spotty beard, stops and notices me. I take a step back. He powers off his drill and the others follow suit.

Eight eyes refuse to blink as they stare at me.

They recognize me, and the pale, sunken skin of their faces chills me. Drained mystics. They're everywhere.

I look across the bridges around me and see no one. There is no one here but these sad-looking men and me. I've lost Davida.

I turn around immediately and head home.

"How was dinner?" asks my mother, seated on the black leather sofa of our living area. Her face is freshly scrubbed, hair still wet from the shower. She is wearing a thick pink robe and sipping from a glass tumbler. All the curtains are drawn, and the overhead lights are dimmed.

Was she waiting up for me?

Klartino has left—after chastising me in the lobby for making him wait so long—and I wasn't expecting a conversation with my mother. "Fine," I lie.

She arches an eyebrow. "Just fine?"

"Nice," I say, correcting myself. "It was very nice."

"Good." She crosses her legs. "You should get to sleep, Aria.

Don't forget that you're filming an ad for the campaign in the morning."

"What?"

"Didn't Thomas tell you about it?"

"No." I squeeze my clutch, thinking of the locket inside. "He didn't."

"There was an explosion earlier tonight on the Lower East Side. A . . . *demonstration* arranged by those damned rebels."

"There was an explosion?" I ask in shock.

She swirls the liquid in her glass. "Yes. We need to take advantage of the timing. We're going to run ads of you and Thomas down at the wreckage, and also one of Garland working with some of the firemen. The poor fools in the Depths may think they're doing themselves a favor by supporting that . . . *mystic* . . . but they couldn't be more wrong. And we won't let her win."

"How many people died?"

My mother takes a swallow of her drink. "Does it matter? Those idiots think they're rallying the poor, but they're only reminding the public how very dangerous mystics are. The rebels will never stop. They need to be exterminated."

I'm speechless, numb. She could at least *pretend* to be sad that innocent people lost their lives. I start to head up the stairs and into my room.

"Aren't you forgetting something?" my mother asks.

I tilt my head, confused.

She bats her eyelids. "Kiss goodnight?"

I force myself to peck her on the cheek. Her skin is ice cold. "Good night."

"Oh, Aria, send Davida down, would you? I have a few things I need her to do."

I can't do this, of course, because Davida is not here. The last thing I want to do is get her in trouble. "Um, I sent her out."

My mother looks genuinely shocked. "You did?"

"Yes, I wanted her to . . . fix the clasp on one of my bracelets." I press my lips together. "It broke."

She glances at her watch. "You sent her out this late? It's past ten."

It's implausible, I know, but all I can do is nod and hope she believes me.

Surprisingly, she does. "I'm glad to see you're finally *using* our servants properly. It's about time. Soon you'll be running a household of your own." She finishes her drink in one large gulp. "Send Magdalena down instead. And be quiet—your father is already asleep."

Kyle is waiting for me at the top of the stairs with his arms crossed.

"Hey," I say. "What are you doing?"

"Heading over to Bennie's," he says.

I try to move past him, but he's like a barricade in a navy-blue T-shirt and jeans. His hair is perfectly messy, as though he's spent a great deal of effort in front of the mirror trying to make it seem like he didn't try at all. Personally, I think it's nice that after all this time dating, he still wants to impress Bennie.

"*You* sent *Davida* out on an errand?" he asks. "I don't believe you. That would be like Kiki buying something on sale."

"I don't care if you believe me or not," I tell him. "Now move."

He doesn't. "You never ask Davida to do anything for you. You hardly even bother Magdalena. Why now?"

"I ask her to do tons of stuff."

"No," he says. "You don't. Now where is she really?"

"Like I told Mom, getting my bracelet fixed."

Kyle takes a step closer. "Which bracelet?"

I take too long before answering, and he laughs. "I'm onto you," Kyle whispers before stepping aside. I don't look back as I pass him.

Instead of changing out of my clothes, I wait for Kyle to leave. Then I sneak into Davida's room.

Davida lives in the servants' wing of our penthouse, on the opposite end of the second floor from where my bedroom is.

I haven't been in Davida's room in months—maybe even years—but her neatness doesn't surprise me. The furnishings are simple and the décor is practically nonexistent: white walls, gray carpet, a narrow bed, and a tall dresser. A small closet and one window that overlooks the Hudson. The only thing that seems personalized is the stitching on her curtains. I walk over to take a closer look: tiny stars fashioned from silver thread, moons and planets intricately designed in red and blue.

Where would Davida keep something private, like a journal?

I sift through the outfits in her closet. Most are versions of her uniform, plus a few bland tops she's allowed to wear out on her days off.

It's not that I don't trust Davida. It's just that—well, I'm suspicious. Dirt from the Depths on the fingertips of her gloves, and now this: sneaking off in the night. What is she not telling me?

I feel around in the gloom under her bed and catch my thumb on the pointed edge of a metal box. I grab either side of it and pull until the thing is in full sight. The box is long enough to store a rifle, like the ones my father keeps in a glass case in his library. There are two clasps. I undo them, lift the lid, and peer inside.

Inside are some of the birthday gifts I have given Davida over the years: an aMuseMe with her favorite songs already downloaded, tiny porcelain dolls with beautifully etched faces, a bounty of jeweled rings and necklaces, an electronic reader with some of my favorite books.

And gloves.

Dozens upon dozens of gloves, all black, neatly folded and stacked in pairs. They look as though they've never been worn—impeccably clean and pressed, no lines or creases.

I pick up a pair and study them: they are linked together by a tiny metal clasp, which I unhook. They feel odd, soft yet durable, as though you could drag a knife across the palm and the material wouldn't tear. The oddest thing about them, though, are the fingertips, each of which is decorated with almost imperceptible circular whorls that I've never noticed before.

I slip one on, and it fits perfectly. I flex my hands and the fingertip whorls immediately start to warm, filling my entire body with a subtle, inexplicable kind of heat.

I extend my hand and stare: What *are* these?

I rip off the glove and fix it back to its partner. I might as well keep them for a little while—there are so many pairs, Davida will never know if one is missing.

Then I pack up everything as it was and leave.

Back in my room, I tuck the gloves and my clutch safely in the back of my armoire.

After a hot bath, I dress in a worn flannel nightgown and press off my bedroom lights. Then I press open the curtains and watch as the city slowly comes into view. The mystic spires are alight with flashes of color. I study them, hoping their oscillation will soothe me to sleep: white to yellow to green.

The change of colors is so fast it'd be easy to miss. But I've been looking at these spires for years.

Eventually I slip underneath my covers, close my eyes, and wait for sleep to overtake me.

"Come," he says, taking my hand as we move in the moonlight—away from the noises of the main canal, onto a narrow street barely wide enough for us to walk side by side.

Reflections of the buildings appear on the water. We run over a tiny bridge. He is in front of me, his hair whipping in the wind.

"Wait!"

"There's no time. They're after us."

He turns to me. I expect to see Thomas's face—only I don't. I see nothing more than a dark circle, covered in a veil of fog.

"Thomas? Is that you?"

"I'm here." He reaches out and pulls me to him. "Don't worry."

I frantically try to wipe away the fog. But the more I try to see him, the darker he becomes, until he's barely there at all, until he's nothing more than a shadow.

· VIII ·

"The mystics will ruin us all!" I scream, clinging to Thomas for dear life and pointing at the man with the sallow skin.

"Cut!"

As soon as the cameras stop rolling, a crew of makeup artists rush over to me, blotting the sweat from my cheeks.

Thomas keeps his arm around me, and I survey the scene of the crime.

The rebel demonstration from the previous night has taken out an entire skyscraper. Explosives were detonated from inside—they shot upward, slicing through the building from the Depths to the Aeries. Thankfully, the occupants were mostly commercial; the only folks who lived there were the poor in the Depths, and it seems they'd been given warning and evacuated. Since the damage was done at night, everyone in the Aeries had already gone home. The explosion was mostly for show.

Unfortunately, thirty floors from the top, the walls burst and toppled over onto one of the connective bridges, snapping the wire cables and crushing a family of five who were heading home from dinner.

"Aria," calls the director of the ad. He saunters over to where Thomas and I are standing—on a bridge perpendicular to the damaged one.

"Yes?"

The director, Kevan-Todd, wipes the top of his shaved head and frowns. "I didn't find your fear believable."

I slip off the mask I'm forced to wear to protect me from the still-settling debris. From a distance, my mother and some city officials look on, craning their necks to see if there's a problem. I want to say that this is ridiculous. There's an actor named James pretending to be a mystic, his body lathered in foundation to make him look sickly, and Kevan-Todd is worried that *I'm* not believable. But I know the ad is important to the campaign, so I get ready for another take.

Thomas squeezes my hand, trying to comfort me. "I'm sorry," I say. "I guess I'm just nervous."

"Why don't you pretend the camera is your best friend?" Kevan-Todd suggests. "And you're just having a casual conversation."

I lift an eyebrow. "A casual conversation about an explosion?"

Thomas lets out a sigh. "Aria."

"All right, all right," I say, slipping the mask back on. "I'll try harder."

Kevan-Todd whips his head around to the rest of the crew. "Okay, guys. Take nine. And let's fix the body bags, hmm? We want them to look like real dead bodies, not deflated donuts."

One of the men rushes over to a group of long black duffels, punching them on the sides to make them seem fuller. I'm not sure what's in them, but the people who actually died last night are already in the crematorium. Later today, their ashes will be scattered in the canals, which is where most people dispose of their loved ones.

"Aaannd . . . action!"

The cameras pan over the wreckage of the building and the bridge, then focus on Thomas. "I'm Thomas Foster," he says in a slick voice, "and this is my fiancée, Aria Rose. Last night, a mystic explosion took the lives of an innocent family. This is exactly the sort of wicked terrorist bombing that our two families have joined together to put an end to. If elected mayor, my brother, Garland, will fight to keep the Aeries safe. To keep *you* safe."

He pauses, and I wait for him to continue. Kevan-Todd waves his hands frantically, and I realize that I've nearly missed my cue.

"The *mystics* will ruin us *all!*"

Then I faint into Thomas's arms.

"Cut!" Kevan-Todd hollers. He shoots me a tepid smile. "Well . . . that's a wrap!"

Thomas yanks off his mask. "Nice job, sweetie." He kisses my cheek. "I'm going to get some water. You want any?"

"Sure," I say, distracted by the screams coming from the opposite bridge, where a slew of teenagers have gathered to watch the filming. Thankfully, they've been contained and the area we're in is secure, but I can hear their shouts:

"Aria! We love you!"

"Thomas is so hot!"

"I want to marry you both!"

I have to laugh because I'm so embarrassed. I've always been in the public eye, but I've never felt like a celebrity before. Two girls wave handmade banners that read:

FORBIDDEN LOVE FOREVER!

It flatters *and* worries me that our romance is more important to people in the Aeries than an explosion. Than death.

I motion to Thomas, wanting to know what he makes of all this attention, only he's off chatting with some girls who have VIP passes and are holding out TouchMes for him to sign electronically.

My mother approaches and gives me a pat on the shoulder. "You were . . . good, Aria." She squeezes out the compliment as if saying it were physically painful. "The ad should be ready to run by the end of the week. We're going to play it in the Depths, make sure that as many people down there see it as possible."

Few of the poor can afford their own television sets, so the city has installed jumbo screens in certain high-traffic areas down below for government announcements. I guess those screens will also broadcast the ad.

"I'm going to Olive and Pimentos for a fitting," Mom continues. "My outfit for the rehearsal dinner is done. Or so I've been told." She rolls her eyes. "You never know with these people. Would you like to come with me?"

I glance back at Thomas, who's still signing autographs. He and Garland are heading to an election strategy meeting soon, and I'd prefer not to be stuck alone with my mother.

Especially when I'm planning to sneak back down to the Depths.

"Actually, I promised I'd meet Kiki for lunch."

"I'd rather you not," she says with a toss of her head. "There's no one to chaperone you; Klartino and Stiggson are on business with your father."

"But I don't need a chaperone."

"That was before," my mother says.

"Before what?"

She tilts her head. "Do you really need me to spell it out for you, Aria? Before you *snuck out* after *overdosing*!"

"Mom, I'm sorry. Really." I give her a pleading look. "Besides, Kiki and I are planning the *wedding*!" It's surprising how easy it is to make up stories for my mother. "She's promised to help me figure out who my bridesmaids should be—God knows I can't remember enough to know who should stand with me."

My mother rests her palm against my cheek. "Poor thing. A little wedding planning is probably just what you need." She looks around, as if convincing herself that there are no lurking dangers, then smiles warmly. "Just be sure you're back in time for dinner with the governor. You know how your father hates for his children to be late!"

Apparently, I need to feign excitement for wedding planning more often. I feel bad for lying to her, but not *too* bad. I kiss her cheek, then say a quick goodbye to Thomas and strike off for the light-rail, waving until they're out of sight.

And then I'm off to the Magnificent Block.

The gondolier pulls up to one of the blue-and-white hitching posts that dot the edges of all the canals, and the boat automatically stops. "Here you are, miss," the old man says, looping a rope around the post and dragging the gondola against the elevated sidewalk.

If he recognizes me, he doesn't mention it. I've brushed my hair out to cover my face as much as I can, but I'm still wearing my dress from the filming: yellow jersey studded with Swarovski crystals, a thick turquoise belt with a silver buckle, and high-heeled sandals that tie around my ankles. I am slightly worried that I'm being tracked, but so far I've been lucky. Either no one has cared to check any of the POD transit histories as of late, or I have my very own Grid guardian angel.

I'd put my money on the former.

Everything in the Depths is much different in the daylight: the water is dingier and browner, the stench—like rotting fish—worse than I remember, the people oddly cheerier. The streets and raised walkways are aswarm with men and women hustling to and fro with bundles under their arms and children attached to their hands. I hop out of the boat and onto a set of cracked steps. It's so hot you could fry an egg on my skin.

"Thank you," I say, dropping a few coins into the gondolier's palm.

A few feet ahead, I see the awning of Java River and step inside.

The old-fashioned bell on the door jingles. People turn to look, then go back to their cups of coffee and plates of sweets. I warm at the sight—the large booths and framed pictures on the walls, the glass case filled with baked goods near the register, the waitress with a piercing in her nostril who served me and Hunter the other night.

I sit down in one of the empty booths. "What can I get you?" the waitress asks.

"Water." Before she can walk away, I add, "And I have a question."

"Well?" she says, tapping one shoe on the tile. "I don't got all day."

I clear my throat. "I was here the other night, with a boy." She stares at me blankly. "A boy named Hunter. He has, um, sort of blondish hair. Kinda rough-looking, but very handsome. Not a model, but—you know . . . modelesque?"

After a moment or so, she rolls her eyes and says, "I don't remember any guy like that. And I don't remember you."

Then she walks away.

I get up and follow her. She disappears into the kitchen, however, so I ask the woman at the register the same thing.

"We were here the other night," I repeat, trying to grab the attention of the older woman, the one with the knotted hair whose skin is covered in liver spots.

"No, you weren't," the woman says while using a rag to wipe the counter clean. "If you know what's good fer you, leave right now. And don't come back, you hear?"

"I don't understand," I say. "I'm just looking for some information about the boy I was with. Hunter. Where I can find him."

The woman grits her teeth. "I told you, girl. I never seen you, nor no boy named Hunter. Understand? Now git." She points to the door of the shop. "Git."

Outside, I blot my forehead with an embroidered handkerchief and search for an open gondola.

The raised sidewalk is mere feet from a canal. A few people are sitting and eating sandwiches, dangling their feet over the water. Down the road, at one of the docks, a line of men and women wait for the water taxi, a boat that holds around fifty people and navigates some of the larger canals. It's cheaper than a gondola, but I can't afford to be recognized by so many people. I haven't been here long; I still have a decent amount of time to get home, shower, and be ready for dinner.

For a moment, I feel a sense of calm—the Depths are less scary during the daytime. I notice the colors of the buildings: faded pink and watery blue, gray and brown and white. Some are decorated with columns, now old and crusty, or carvings of cherubs' faces, which are falling apart. They're almost charming.

I walk down the sidewalk, away from the dock, and look at some of the hitching poles jutting out of the water, hoping a gondolier has roped in, but I don't see any. A string of ratty-looking children push past, nearly knocking me to the ground. "Hey, watch where you're going!" I yell, but no one seems to hear me. Or care.

And then I feel a tap on my shoulder.

I whirl around to see a girl about my age standing before me. She has short brown hair cut just above her shoulders, with eyes of the same color, and she's wearing a dress that seems two sizes too big. Her skin is pale, almost white, and she has the telltale sign of mystic drainings: yellow-green circles underneath her eyes.

"You're not crazy." Taking my arm, she pulls me down a

deserted alleyway that's a bit darker and cooler thanks to the shade of the tall buildings.

"I'm Tabitha." She sticks out her hand.

I take it in mine. Her grip is surprisingly light. Frail. "I'm—"

"Aria Rose," she says. "I know. I work in the back at Java River. I'm . . . a friend of Turk's."

My eyes widen at his name. "So you remember me?"

"Look, I can't say much, but I can tell you how to find Hunter." She raises her thin arm and points down the alleyway. In the distance, I can see a mystic spire rising above the rest of the buildings. Even in the daytime, it is extraordinarily bright. "Follow the lights," she says cryptically, in a hushed voice.

I wait for her to explain, but she doesn't.

"What do you mean?" I ask. "The lights are on poles. They don't *lead* anywhere."

Tabitha glances around nervously. "They do if you know how to read them," she says. "They're not steady. The way they pulse? All the colors? It means something."

I think back to last night, when I was watching the lights flicker from my bedroom window. "So you're saying there's a pattern? How the lights work . . . it's not random?"

Tabitha nods fervently. "The spires hold mystic energy, which is *alive*—it can speak to those who know how to listen."

"No offense, but I don't understand what this has to do with me. Or Hunter."

"Our energy is part of how we communicate," Tabitha says. "How we tell people things that can't be spoken aloud." She cranes her neck to see if we've been noticed. "Normally, two mystics can communicate without talking through a simple touch. I no longer have that ability—that's what happens when we're drained. They use some of the energy to fuel the city and store the extra in the spires."

"Why do they drain more energy than they need?"

She shrugs her bony shoulders. "Power. And money. What else is there?"

"Money . . . what do you mean?"

Tabitha tilts her head. "Stic, obviously. Manhattan has one of the biggest mystic populations in the States. Stic is made from drained mystic energy, then sold illegally all over the world." She looks at me as if I should know better. "Think about it, Aria."

But I don't want to. Who cares if people sell Stic? I've been taught that mystics are dangerous, the mortal enemies of non-mystics, and that their deepest desire is to kill me and everyone else in the Aeries. I was taught that the mystics were responsible for the Mother's Day Conflagration.

How much of that is true?

"Look," Tabitha says, glancing nervously down the alleyway. "Forget all that for now. If you can understand the energy, it will show you how to find Hunter."

"But I'm not a mystic. I don't know *how* to read the energy from the spires. Can't you just tell me where he is?"

Tabitha shakes her head rapidly. "No," she says. "The rebels would kill me if I led you to them."

"They'd *kill* you? Then why are you even telling me any of this?"

"Because," she says, her voice softening. "I can tell you love him."

Now it's my turn to shake my head. "Hunter? I don't love him," I say. "I barely know him. I'm engaged—to someone else."

"Then why are you trying to find him?"

"It's complicated." I look away, wondering how much I should reveal. "I had an accident. And now I'm supposed to be married in a month and I can't remember my fiancé. I've been having strange dreams. I thought maybe Hunter could help me."

Tabitha listens quietly as I speak. Then she leans in and says, "You don't need Hunter to help you with that."

"I don't?"

"No. You need Lyrica."

"I'm sorry—who?"

"Lyrica." Tabitha spews out an address. "If anyone can help you, she can." She turns and says, "They'll have noticed that I left by now. I've got to go." A cough racks her skinny frame. "Wait until dark, then follow the lights. Trust me. You'll find your answers."

At dinner that night, I eat like a proper lady, as always, the way I have been taught.

Kyle rolls his eyes at me across the table, and even then I do not laugh. I am on my best behavior. I listen quietly as my parents discuss politics with the governor.

"Johnny, do you really think this mystic Violet Brooks has a chance?" the governor asks.

My father is silent, then says, "Yes."

The word sounds deadly coming from his mouth. What would happen if Violet did win the election, if some of my father's stronghold over the city was diminished? Would my parents still want me to marry Thomas?

After our main course—rack of lamb, fresh asparagus, and wasabi mashed potatoes—Governor Boch asks why I've been so quiet. "You've always been quite the chatterbox," he says.

I fake a yawn. "Excuse me. I'm just tired."

"Aria filmed a campaign spot this morning," my mother chimes in. "She was *very* effective." Is this her way of trying to be nice? "How was your lunch with Kiki?" she asks, playing with one of her rings, a ruby set in yellow gold. Nothing about my mother is subtle—the blouse she's wearing tonight has fur trim on the sleeves. Only someone like my mother would wear fur in one of the hottest cities in the world.

"It was fun. We picked the bridesmaids for the wedding. Five of them." I'll have to ask Kiki to cover for me. And help me come up with names for bridesmaids.

"That's wonderful, dear."

Kyle is busy texting someone, his phone hidden in his lap. My father just stares at me, his dark eyes fixed on mine.

"Do you have any questions about the election I can help answer?" Governor Boch asks, sipping from his wineglass. He's finished nearly an entire bottle by himself—his lips have taken on a dark purple stain. "I'd be happy to."

"Actually, I do have one," I say. My father raises his thick eyebrows. "Why are more mystics drained than are needed to fuel the city?"

The governor sputters as he's swallowing his wine, making a choking sound.

Kyle leans over and smacks him on the back. "All clear," Kyle says loudly.

"Aria!" my mother says. "What kind of question is that for the governor?"

"A legitimate one," I say. "Isn't it?"

My father raises his knife and points it directly at me. "*That's enough,* Aria." He waits a moment, then slams the knife back down on the table. "What are you going to do before the wedding? Mope around here all summer and ask ridiculous questions? You have an entire year before you enter university. What's your plan?"

I choose not to answer him. The silence is deafening.

"Well?" he says.

"I could get a job," I hear myself saying.

"Aria, be serious." My mother lets out a laugh.

"I *am* serious!" I say. I've never worked before, of course, but it suddenly feels like the perfect way to escape my parents. If I had a job, I'd have a reason to leave the apartment every day.

Kyle stops texting long enough to chime in. "The only thing Aria is qualified to do is shop and hang out with Kiki. And the last time I checked, neither of those are *jobs.*"

"Like *you've* ever been employed?" I retort. *"Please."*

"Surprise, surprise, Aria—you're wrong. As usual," Kyle says. "I worked for Dad two summers ago. I was Eggs's assistant."

Dad chuckles, but my mother *tsk-tsk*s. "Kyle, I told you not to call him that." She turns to the governor, who looks confused. "When Kyle was young, he loved to have eggs Benedict for breakfast. He's since taken to referring to Patrick Benedict as Eggs." She dabs the corners of her lips with a napkin. "It's highly disrespectful," Mom says to Kyle. "You're far too much of a gentle-man for that."

I start to object about Kyle being a gentleman, then decide to appeal to my father instead. "If Kyle has had work experience, why can't I? I'd do anything—sort mail, answer phones, whatever."

I don't know much about Benedict, only that he's a reformed mystic who is now a stalwart Rose supporter and does something associated with regulating mystic energy. He's the only mystic I've ever seen my father speak to, let alone trust.

"But Aria," my mother protests. "What would people say? Besides, you have the wedding to think about—there's so much to do!"

"That's why we have a wedding planner," I say. "Actually, that's why we have *three* wedding planners—you should know, you chose them yourself."

"I so wanted *four,* but Johnny put his foot down," my mother says to the governor. "Weddings can be so tiring, and I do hate odd numbers."

"I don't know much about weddings, Melinda," the governor says, holding up his ringless hand. "I've been a bachelor all my life."

My mother takes a quick sip of her wine. "How tragic."

"Maybe if I had a job," I continue, looking down, pretending to be suddenly sad, "I wouldn't worry so much about the wedding. And my memory problems."

It's a dirty move, I know, but at this point I'm sure my parents will do anything if they think it'll make me go along with the marriage.

Dad's bottom lip quivers, which means he's actually considering my proposition. "Fine," he says after what feels like a lifetime. "I'll call Patrick in the morning. Having to be answerable to somebody else for a change might actually do you some good."

Mom frowns, but I don't care. For the first time in what feels like forever, I give my father a real smile.

And much to my surprise, he smiles back.

Before I go to sleep, I stare once again out my bedroom windows, this time with new knowledge of the mystic spires.

They're still enigmas. Energy shoots through them like an electric current. Bright yellow. Hot white. Electric green. The colors flow together so smoothly they seem like one continuous stream.

I glance at my clock, then back out the window, focusing on one spire. There is a flash of yellow—four seconds. A burst of white— six seconds. The ripple of green is the shortest—two seconds.

What does that mean?

I look to the right, where a different spire is nestled between two skyscrapers along the Hudson. I time this one as well. The pulse here changes at a slower rate—yellow radiates for ten seconds, then white for ten seconds. No hint of green.

Tabitha told me to listen. But what in the Aeries am I listening for?

PART TWO

Love will not be spurred
to what it loathes.

—SHAKESPEARE

Making Love, Not War

These days, getting cozy with your sworn enemy is all the rage.

By now, everyone knows the story of Aria Rose and Thomas Foster's secret romance—how they defied their parents and fell in love. But unlike Romeo and Juliet, this pair of New York City lovers is getting their happy ending: a wedding at the end of the summer, just after the August 21 mayoral election in which Thomas's older brother, Garland Foster, is running against registered mystic Violet Brooks.

The teen lovebirds have been mum on any details, leading us all to wonder: How did they meet? How did they convince their parents—whose political rivalry dates back to the early twentieth century—to let them be together?

"Forbidden love has been around since the beginning of time," says Professor Jinner of West University. "It's a theme we've seen in the earliest plays and books."

Then why is everyone so obsessed with Aria and Thomas?

"I'm fourteen years old and I've never even been to

the East Side," says Talia St. John, whose family supports the Roses. "But now my mom says we can go. There are probably so many cute boys over there, and now I get to meet them! Everything is changing, and I like it."

Well put, Talia.

But seriously—the union of Aria Rose and Thomas Foster will erase the invisible dividing line that has marked our city for years. And most people see this as a good thing.

Aria and Thomas, no strangers to the flashes of paparazzi cameras, have frequently been photographed on both Manhattan's East and West sides.

"They're showing that two people really can make a difference," says Talia.

And let's face the truth: it doesn't hurt that they're both gorgeous.

Thomas, with his movie star looks, has been making girls all over the city swoon for years. And Aria has the classic features of a storybook princess.

Plus, they really do seem to be *in love*. Even a simple touch of his hand on her back shows how taken Manhattan's no-longer-so-eligible bachelor is with his bride-to-be.

Perhaps even more remarkable is the number of Aeries couples who have admitted to having their very own star-crossed romances—former Rose and Foster supporters who have joined together, putting aside their past differences to unite against the mystic threat.

"I never thought we'd be able to marry," says Franklin Viofre, a Rose supporter who's been having a secret affair with Melissa Taylor, a Foster supporter. "But now that Thomas and Aria are showing everyone that this is okay, I proposed. And she said yes!"

Not everyone is happy with the changes, of course. There have been small protests from those on both sides who seek to keep things the way they've always been: separate. "No good will come from this union," says an anonymous source close to the Fosters. "Mark my words."

Only time will tell. But for now, let's celebrate.

—from the *Manhattan View,* an Aeries society e-column

· IX ·

"Earth to Aria? Hello?"

I look up from my TouchMe. Kiki and Bennie are staring at me like I'm a creature from another planet.

"Can't you actually *break* during your lunch break?" Kiki motions to her half-eaten chopped salad, then to the dining area of Paolo's, the restaurant in the government building where I've been working for the past two weeks. "What's so important that you can't focus on us for an hour?"

"A *half* hour," I say. "Sorry. Work is just a lot more . . . work than I expected."

Filing, getting coffee, and basically being Benedict's unpaid assistant is far from glamorous. And while it does get me out of the house every day and away from my mother's hawk eyes, I am totally and completely bored.

"Well, tell us about it!" Bennie says. Today she reminds me of a child—her dark hair is pulled back into a ponytail, and she's wearing a pastel blue-and-green day dress. "You basically fell off the Aeries—I have no idea what you've been up to, other than the pics I've seen of you and Thomas online. Somebody's been getting some action! And by action I mean *tongue* action."

"Seriously," Kiki says. "Haven't you ever heard of getting a room?"

I roll my eyes. "It's all for show, guys."

The girls exchange a confused look.

"I mean . . . it's important for us to look like we're in love," I clarify. "Important for the election."

I think back to the other night, when Thomas and I went out to dinner on the Lower East Side and had our picture taken outside the restaurant; how his arm fit snugly around my waist as he pulled me close to him, how his breath smelled like the cinnamon gum he was chewing as he leaned down to kiss my cheek. How I felt like, for a split second, maybe this was meant to be—until one of the paps yelled, "On the lips, guys!"

"So does that mean you *are* in love?" Kiki takes another bite of her salad, then stares at me cryptically. "That you remember?"

Her question makes me tense—and upset. The only possible memories I have are weird dreams where I can't see Thomas's face. I know Kiki wants me to confide in her. But I have nothing to say about Thomas, and with Hunter, well . . . I don't think even *she* would understand that. "Can we talk about something else?"

"Sure," Bennie says, sensing that I'm uncomfortable. "What's your schedule like—from start to finish. Go!"

"Well . . . I get up every morning—"

"Duh!" Kiki interjects.

"—and brush my teeth and shower—"

"Aria! Get to the good stuff!"

"Fine, fine," I say, chuckling. "My dad and I ride the rail together—"

"How's that?"

"We don't talk much. Light stuff—the weather, the wedding. His office is in the same building on the top floor but I rarely see him during the day. Mostly I'm just the office bitch. I get water and coffee for people when they want it, organize some of the older filing systems, and process the mystic draining reports. It's pretty boring, actually."

Bennie takes a sip of her Diet Coke. "Have you made any friends?"

I think about the people who work on the floor with me. They're all much older, and while everyone is pretty nice, it's fake nice—I know it's only because of who I am. "Not really. I miss you guys."

"We miss you, too!" Kiki cries. "Why don't you just quit? Wouldn't it be more fun to hang out with us?"

"I *am* hanging out with you," I reply, motioning to the table.

Kiki waves her hand. "You should be hanging out with us *all the time*. Yesterday we got mani-pedis at that spa downtown that we love, and while the woman was painting my nails I just started crying, because all I could think was *Aria* loves *to get her nails painted*." She sniffles. "This is our last summer before you get married, Aria, and then everything will be different."

I start to say that nothing will change when I'm married, but in my heart I know that isn't true. "I can't quit. But I'll definitely make more time for us to hang out."

"Good," Bennie says, smiling at me. "You can start this weekend."

"What's this weekend?" I ask, knowing that Thomas will likely want to spend time with me.

Kiki stares me down. "You can spend *one* night away from Thomas." There's an edge to her voice that surprises me, and I wonder if she's still upset about the affair and the overdose. Not necessarily that they happened, but that she wasn't privy to them before anyone else was.

"What's that supposed to mean?"

"I miss you," she says. "You see him, like, practically every night. What happened to girls' night? Gossiping, watching crappy TV, trying on each other's bras. . . ."

"We never tried on each other's bras," I say. "That's weird."

"I don't mean *literally*," Kiki says. "It's an expression. I think. Regardless, we used to do everything together, Aria. Now . . . it's like I barely know you."

"Fine," I say. "Let's have a girls' night."

"No!" Bennie shouts. Kiki and I look at her, confused. "I mean . . . I'm having a little soiree. My parents are vacationing in Brazil. It's the perfect excuse to do something fun." Bennie immediately begins texting. "Don't mind me. I'm just setting reminders to hire a caterer, and maybe a DJ . . . oh and we'll need a few bartenders, too—"

"Whoa there," I say. "Why don't we just have a small get-together? Us girls?"

"Stop being so selfish!" Kiki's face is getting flushed; she unbuttons one of the buttons on her blue Oxford shirt and fans herself with her napkin. "I want some action! Some romance! You're both in relationships, and I've got no one," she says, pouting. "I just want a boy to kiss me. Is that too much to ask? Kiss me with some tongue."

Bennie thinks for a moment. "Don't worry, Kiks. I'll ask Kyle to bring along some of his friends. There was this boy in his literature course last semester I always thought was sexy in a, you know, collegiate kind of way. Brown hair, brown eyes—"

"Oh, I just *love* the color brown," Kiki chimes in.

"—and I think his name is Don Marco," Bennie says. "Or maybe it's Paul. I can't remember. Anyway, this will be so much fun!" She stops texting and looks up at me. "I'm going to invite a few people from the Foster side. Is that all right?"

I think of Gretchen Monasty, how she told me at the plummet that some things should just remain separate. Well, screw Gretchen. "Sure, Bennie. Whatever you like."

She grins. "It'll be, like, the first time kids from both sides are hanging out together. The blending has got to start *somehow,* and a party is as good an event as any, right? Just make sure you, like, grind up on Thomas in front of everyone. Show people that true love is what it's all about!" She glances back down. "Ugh. My to-do list is already huge. I need some major assistance."

"I'll do whatever I can to help," Kiki says, looking to me as if to say, *Will you?*

Before I can respond, my TouchMe buzzes. There's a text on the screen from Patrick Benedict:

YOU'RE LATE

"Girls, I gotta go." I motion for the waiter and ask him to put the bill on my tab.

"Will you be there this weekend?" Bennie asks. There's a hopefulness in her voice that I don't want to squash, and I find myself saying yes.

"I guess that'll have to do . . ." Kiki says. It feels like her green eyes see right through me. "For *now*. Don't think I'm not planning you a kick-ass bridal shower, fool."

The office itself is on the two hundredth floor of the Rivington building, just above Fortieth Street on the West Side, about thirty blocks from our apartment. This part of the city used to be called Hell's Kitchen, before the Conflagration. Now it's Rose headquarters.

I say goodbye to Kiki and Bennie, then walk through the body scanner in the lobby and am granted access. It's two p.m., which means that it's time for my afternoon coffee round.

After I take the elevator, I walk down the hallway, passing Benedict's office and those of some of the other executives, and a stainless steel door without a keyhole or a touchpad. I'm not sure what it's for, and nobody else seems to know, either. Then the hallway opens into a maze of cubicles, which is where I work.

I slip off my cardigan and hang it over the side of the cube I've been assigned. Near me are twenty other desks, spread out evenly. The stack of manila envelopes on my desk has piled so high I fear it will topple over. *Mental note: Get on those.* They're copies of the draining reports from over ten years ago, before everything was streamlined electronically. I have to transfer all the data onto the TouchMe system, but it's taking longer than I expected.

I hope Benedict doesn't yell at me.

"Eleanor, would you like any coffee?" I ask the woman at the cube next to me. She's in her midthirties, with straight blond hair that is so glossy it hurts my eyes.

"A mocha," she replies, *"nonfat."* She speaks to me as though I'm hard of hearing. "As in, without any fat."

"Right. Anything else?"

"It's just that yesterday my mocha had fat in it. As in the milk was at least two percent."

Despite her actual words, I'm pretty sure what she means is *You're dumb and I hate you.*

I just nod and repeat, "Nonfat."

"Steve," I say, heading south, where a man with a yellow-and-pink striped tie is perched at his desk, pecking at his TouchMe and occasionally letting out a high-pitched giggle. "Coffee?"

"Hazelnut. Iced." His voice is monotone, almost robotic. "Large. Sugar," he says without even looking at me.

"Okaaay," I say, backing up and continuing to make the rounds. I even write the requests down on a notepad to make sure I don't forget any.

Marlene four desks down orders an Americano, no sugar.

Robert at the far end of the floor asks for a tea, not coffee. "My stomach can't handle the acid," he says.

I take the rest of the inner office's orders, then head back into the hallway where the private offices are. I'll save Benedict for last, since he tends to yell rather than speak. He's the only person here who doesn't seem intimidated by my last name—likely because he works so closely with my father and already knows he's on Dad's good side.

I jot down a few more orders—two regular coffees, one pistachio muffin, and an iced cappuccino—before I knock tentatively on Elissa Genevieve's door.

"Elissa?" I say.

"Come in!"

The door retracts and I walk into Elissa's office, which is painted a sunny yellow. The room is free of clutter, containing only her oblong desk and a narrow bookshelf.

"Aria," she says, seeming genuinely happy to see me. "How are you?" She points to one of the empty chairs by her desk.

"Thanks," I say, taking a seat.

I like Elissa. She's the only person in the office who seems real to me. She works with Benedict, monitoring the city's mystic energy, but I don't hold that against her. They're nothing at all alike: Benedict is short-tempered and harsh, barking out orders around the office like a drill sergeant, while Elissa speaks in soothing, even tones and stops by my cubicle at least once or twice a day to see how I'm doing.

"Good afternoon?"

"It's okay," I say. "How about you?"

Elissa shrugs. She's wearing a smart-looking navy suit with a cream-colored blouse and strappy sandals. Her blond hair is twisted into an elegant chignon, and while her skin is as pale as any drained mystic's, she's somehow able to carry the look well. Looking closely, I can see concealer hiding the bruises underneath her eyes, the blush giving her cheeks a bit more life, but mostly she looks like a striking, beautiful woman—certainly one of the best-looking forty-year-olds I've ever seen.

"Just monitoring the Grid." Elissa swivels her TouchMe so that I can see it. "I'm keeping a close watch for anything strange around the old subway entrances." She points to a few places on the screen where the subways used to be—Ninety-Sixth Street, then Seventy-Second, Forty-Second, Thirty-Fourth, and Fourteenth. "It's rumored that the rebels are living in the old subway tunnels, but we're still looking for a working entrance."

"Well, that sounds a whole lot more interesting than what I've been up to!" I flash my notepad. "Coffee?"

"Everybody's got to start somewhere, Aria." She grins. "No thanks. I saw your friends drop you off after lunch. Did you have fun?"

"Oh. Yeah, we did. Thanks for asking."

"Did you hear about the demonstration this morning?" Elissa asks.

"No! Another one?" The ad I filmed with Thomas started airing last week. I've already seen it more than a dozen times on TV. It was supposed to help *stop* these incidents, not encourage more of them.

"Rebels detonated more explosives, in an office building on the Lower East Side this time. Luckily, the company that used it was in the process of moving, so most of the employees were at the new location. There were only a handful of casualties. But still."

I gulp, immediately thinking of Hunter. Would he ever be part of such a violent act? Would Turk?

"That's why it's so important we find their hideout before they can do any more harm," Elissa says. "I admire their desire for change, but violence is never the way."

"I agree." I think of how my father shot an innocent man simply to prove a point. What would Elissa say about him if she knew that? "'I object to violence because when it appears to do good, the good is only temporary; the evil it does is permanent.'" I feel a little silly to be quoting from my textbooks. "I think Gandhi said that."

Elissa stares right at me. "Interesting." I cringe; something about Elissa makes me feel dumb. In her smart-looking suit, with her perfectly styled hair and flawless skin, she seems like the kind of woman who always knows just what to say.

"You know I'm a reformed mystic, don't you? Both Patrick and I are."

I nod. "You seem . . . healthier than most registered mystics, though."

She laughs. "Well, thank you. I suppose that's one of the plusses of working for your father. Patrick and I are only drained once a year, so we're able to keep up some of our powers and a semblance of regular life. Otherwise, we'd never function at the office." She pauses, looking thoughtful. "That stays between us, though. Okay? Don't go texting it or tweeting or whatever it is you kids do."

"Okay." Elissa is the only one here who pays me any attention. I'm not going to rat her out. "So is that why you're working for my father?"

"That's just a perk. I believe in rules, Aria," Elissa says. "There must be an *order* to things. It's what keeps anarchy at bay. Your father believes that, too. He's a great man. I promise you—Manhattan would be chaotic without men like your father and George Foster. And someday soon, women like you."

"Do you live in the Block?" I ask.

Elissa chuckles. "Heavens, no. I live up here, on the West Side—with all the other Rose supporters."

It's nice how devoted Elissa is to my family, but doesn't she feel conflicted, knowing most of her kind are housed in ghettos in the Depths while the rest of us—including her—float free in the Aeries?

Maybe when I get to know her better, I'll ask her more about her choices. But for now I have to remain Johnny Rose's naive daughter, so as not to raise suspicion.

"What about women like Violet Brooks? She wants rules and order, too—that's what she says, anyway."

Elissa takes in a sharp breath. "Violet Brooks," she says—and I prepare for the condemnation I know is coming—"is a smart woman with good ideas."

"You think so?" That isn't what I was expecting.

"Your father wouldn't like my saying so, but it's true. Unfortunately, she is also a sadly deluded woman who doesn't understand the system. The only thing a mystic mayor can promise Manhattan is misery and death. She's a threat to the safety of the entire city." Elissa leans forward. "That's why we're all so happy about you and Thomas! Once you're married, no mystic will ever have a shot at public office."

"Aria!"

I whip around and see Patrick Benedict charging right toward me. He's a small man, as thin and pliable as a sheet of metal, his expression always sneeringly intelligent. Today he's wearing his typical outfit—a dark suit with a light-colored tie. His thinning black hair is combed back, his thick eyebrows are raised, and the centers of his cheeks are bright red. Like Elissa, he has the pale skin of a drained mystic, only without the circles underneath his eyes or the gaunt, sickly appearance.

"What are you doing? You're supposed to be working, not fraternizing." He narrows his eyes at Elissa. "You should know better, Genevieve."

"Calm down, Patrick," Elissa says. "Aria is doing a good job."

"A good job?" His intonation lets me know he disagrees. "There's a stack of files on her desk that was supposed to have been cleared already. Meanwhile, she's going off to lunch with her friends and chatting with you." Benedict zeroes in on me. "I've told your father about your work ethic, and he's not happy, Aria. He wants to see you. Upstairs."

I want to stand up and smack the smug expression right off Benedict's face. But I know that won't win me any points—with anybody.

"*Now,*" Benedict says.

I wait outside the double doors to my father's office, which occupies the entire top floor of the building. They're made of shiny brass and adorned with metal roses whose edges look sharp enough to draw blood. Two hulking bodyguards with Rose tattoos up their cheeks stand in front of them, arms crossed firmly over their chests. Catherine, my father's secretary, is seated at her desk.

"Aria, he will see you now," Catherine tells me. The bodyguards step aside, pulling the doors open. I give a small curtsey and then stroll past them. The doors close behind me with a soft click.

The air-conditioning sends gooseflesh up and down my arms the moment I cross the threshold—it's even colder in here than in the rest of the building. The far wall is made up entirely of windows looking out on the Hudson. It's the only touch of modernity in the place. Otherwise, it's all mahogany walls and floors, brown leather couches, and overstuffed bookshelves—throwbacks to the nineteenth-century robber baron style.

"Aria," my father says, motioning to a chair across from his desk. "Sit."

He's in a dark suit today, and a navy-blue tie with orange polka dots. He's clean-shaven and his dark eyes have a sparkle in them, nearly as bright as the jewel in the center of the Rose family crest on the ring he wears on his right index finger.

Behind him is a large oil painting in a gilt frame. Impressionist, from the look of it: a golden-orange sunset over the Hudson River. I don't remember seeing it before. I realize it is mystic enhanced, like the paintings in the Fosters' apartment, when the colors turn and begin to glow pink and red, and the thin blue waves of the river rock back and forth.

"Thanks," I say, glancing at the screen of his TouchMe. Dad sees me looking and presses a button; the entire thing goes blank. "You wanted to see me?"

"Why don't you start by telling me why I'm getting complaints about you from Patrick. He says that you're a slow worker, that you're not taking this job seriously."

"I *am* taking it seriously—"

"You *asked* for this opportunity, Aria. You should be doing everything that is requested of you and more. Instead, you're dallying, doing the bare minimum—if that."

"It's not like that, Dad. Benedict has it in for me!"

"No one *has it in* for you," he replies sternly. "If I get another complaint, I'll send you right back home and we'll forget all about this *job* experiment. Do you understand?"

"Yes," I say, because . . . what else is there to say?

Dad stands and motions for me to follow him to the far wall of windows.

"Look out," he tells me. "What do you see?"

I peer out at the other skyscrapers. From here Manhattan looks cold and intimidating, a metropolis of broken-up islands and naked steel, of stone and glass behemoths.

"I see a city," I tell him.

He clucks his tongue. "That is exactly your problem. This is not just a city, Aria. It is *your* city.

"There's a reason why we aren't as close as we once were," he says. "We're so alike, you and I. Your mother and brother are different . . . softer. I remember once, years ago, you were playing with Kiki and fell down and scraped your knees. You didn't cry or call for help. You just wiped the blood off with your hands and continued playing." He smiles at me, a rare genuine smile. "I knew then that you were meant for great things. That underneath your beauty, you were tough. That you would carry on the traditions of our family."

"But we're ending the traditions," I say. "By marrying Thomas, I'll be helping to end them, our feud—all of it."

"Yes."

Suddenly, from somewhere deep inside me, a question bursts forth. "What if I don't want to marry Thomas?" I ask, thinking of the boy in my dreams—whoever he is.

I wait for my father to yell. Or to slap me. He does neither.

Instead, he presses his hands to the glass, spreading his fingers open. "I was young once, Aria, and I had dreams . . . dreams that didn't necessarily coincide with what *my* father wanted for me." Dad's face softens for a moment. "I put my family before myself, and that is how I built my life. There is not a choice when your family is involved." He pauses. "If you do not choose your family, Aria, then we do not choose you. You will be stricken from the record, as if you've never existed."

My lips begin to tremble, and I worry that I might start to cry—and the last thing I want is to show how weak I am.

"Now go," he says, and I don't hesitate. I immediately start walking across the hardwood floor, toward the door.

"Oh, and Aria?" he calls out. I glance at him over my shoulder; he's standing by his desk, resting one hand on his TouchMe.

"Yes?"

"I love you," he says.

· X ·

That evening, when I get home from work, I go straight to my room.

The stink of roses overwhelms me. My bedroom is full of them—Thomas has sent a bouquet to me for every day that I've worked at the office. The cards that accompany them are full of bland professions of love—*I'll be thinking of you with each passing minute,* one says, and another reads *I love you more and more each day.* They're probably written by his assistant.

I've seen him most every night, as well. He comes to the apartment for dinner with us; he talks about politics and the upcoming election with my father while my mother shows me dress swatches and menus for the wedding.

He's taken me to the movies. We've had ice cream together. He's been sweet.

Does it matter if I can't remember how much I love him? Sometimes I look at him and think, *It's a handsome face. It could be the missing face from my dreams—right?*

But my feelings for Thomas are like melting ice. When I try to recall our past, I get nothing more than distorted visions—

half-memories that only leave me more confused. *Remember*, I tell myself, like the note instructed. Like the boy in my dreams has told me. *Remember. Remember. Remember.*

I finish dressing for dinner. My hair has grown longer than I usually keep it, but I don't mind—when it's tied back, in a ribbon, I like how it leaves my face exposed, how the waves fall below my shoulders.

I pull open one of my dresser drawers to root for an Alice band. I move aside a few loose bracelets and some of my tortoiseshell combs, and I see a tear in the drawer lining.

I run a finger over the blue-and-white striped paper. The tear follows one of the blue lines, a cut so minor you can hardly see it. I try to smooth it out with my nail, but when I run my hand over it, I can feel something underneath.

Gently, I grab onto the tear and pull; the paper lifts easily, revealing loose papers. I gather them up and see that they are letters. The one on the top is dated more than six months back.

What are they doing here? I organize them by date and begin reading the oldest one.

It has been three days since we met in the Depths. Three days and all I've been thinking of is you.

I don't even know if this note will reach you, and I don't want to say anything more personal in case it ends up in the wrong hands.

Meet me in the Circle tomorrow night. Please. I just want to look into those starry eyes of yours one more time, and maybe, just maybe, you will want to look into mine, too. (Too corny?)

My breath comes quickly, and I feel a tightening in my chest. I've found a stash of love letters—from Thomas to me!—that I must have hidden away for safety. I pick up the next.

I waited and waited, but you didn't come. This entire week has been miserable. I can't sleep, I can't eat, I drive myself crazy thinking about you. Please, do a guy a favor and just meet me, simply to put me out of my misery?

Tomorrow night, same place? I'll wait until the Circle closes.

I flip to the next one.

You came! I knew you would! I have nothing to say tonight but thank you.

And the next.

It's ridiculous how one encounter can truly change your life. It's been what—a week?—since we met, and you're all I think about. In the morning, when I wake up, I think about your beautiful face, your dark eyes, your skin, your lips . . . and during the day all I hear is the sound of your voice, all I feel is the touch of your hand on my shoulder . . . and at night, I toss and turn, willing myself to fall asleep as quickly as possible so I can dream of you . . . and of us . . . together.

Meet me again? I'll send you directions. And keep checking your balcony for these notes. I don't dare sign my name or give my location outright . . . but we'll come up with a code that works for us, won't we?

Until then.

I clutch the letters to my chest. A relationship is unfolding before my very eyes. Even if I can't remember this happening, all is not lost.

A buzzer sounds.

"Aria!" Magdalena calls over the intercom. "Your mother is waiting for you and your brother to begin dinner!"

"Be right there!" I say into the monitor.

One more, I tell myself.

J—

> *It's an awesome idea to address each other as Romeo and Juliet, star-crossed lovers that we are. I'm so happy I didn't frighten you. I thought telling you the truth—my last name, and who I am—would make you run . . . but you're much stronger than I imagined, and this secret between us will only make us stronger, surer, as sturdy as the Damascus steel that supports our city. There is so much to know, so much to learn. Where do we even begin? I must see you again. Tomorrow? The night after?*
>
> *R*

Romeo and Juliet! This is crazy! It can't be Thomas who was so sensitive, so artful, so—

The buzzer sounds again. "Aria!" Magdalena repeats.

"Coming!" I say, stuffing the letters back inside my drawer. They'll be safe for now. I leave my bedroom, the carpet beneath my feet plush and soft as clouds. I feel happy for the first time in . . . well, a long time, anyway.

Dinner goes by quickly. Kyle never comes down, and my mother natters on about the wedding plans while Bartholomew serves us—caprese salad to start, and a main course of stewed rabbit over fennel, with new potatoes and other things, but I can't seem to focus on any of it, and I eat without seeing what I'm eating. Thomas and my father are off with Garland, doing something election-related that we're not privy to. I can hear Magdalena puttering about in the kitchen. I don't know where Davida is.

Not that any of it matters. All I can think about is the letters. They're my only real clue to the romantic life I had before my overdose.

After an appropriate amount of time, I feign a headache. "May I be excused?"

"Fine," my mother says, distracted by pictures of centerpiece options for the wedding reception. "Make sure your brother knows that he's going to bed without any dinner. This isn't a free-for-all, it's a household."

I leave the table calmly. As soon as I'm out of sight, however, I run upstairs and into my bedroom. I retrieve the letters from my drawer and lie down on my bed, picking up where I left off.

J—

You didn't come last night. I waited and waited. Is there somebody else? If there is . . . my life will be over. Everything was dark before I met you and now there is so much light—I couldn't tolerate being shut back into the darkness. Or maybe you couldn't escape last night—something to do with your father, your brother? Let me know so I won't worry.

Forever yours,

R

I wish I had my responses! I must ask Thomas if he's saved them. Surely he must have.

J—

Thank you for calming me down. I know I can get a little crazy when it comes to seeing you. You're like the antidote to a poison—calming, soothing. You make me feel safe in a world full of chaos.

It's not fair to us, this unnecessary hatred our families have toward each other. And for what? But never mind that for now. Seeing you in the Depths last night, holding your hand, kissing your neck . . . my God, you were on fire. There is nothing mystic light has that you don't have. You burn brighter than anything or anyone else in the entire world.

I'm yours for as long as you will have me.

R

J—

I don't know how much longer I can keep going like this. Are you ready to be honest? I know it frightens you, what might happen if we admit our love, but what's the worst that can happen—our families disown us, and we live a life of poverty, but a life full of love? Or we leave New York entirely and go somewhere else? Sure, we'll have no money, but nothing is as terrible as not being able to love you for the rest of my life. Why wait? Are you unsure of me—of us? Say the word and I'll scream my love for you from the highest points in the Aeries, all the way down to the lowest canals.

I love you.

R

J—

Did my last letter frighten you? Your windows are shut tight . . . have you changed your mind? We can slow down . . . wait to tell our parents . . . I'll do anything for you. Just let me know what's wrong so I can fix it.

R

J—

Your silence is unbearable. I don't know what to think, other than you don't want me anymore . . . or something terrible has happened to you . . . and if either is true, I can't live for one more day. . . . I will come to you tomorrow night . . . please be there.

R

Now that I've read Thomas's words, I can't believe I ever doubted our love. Any superficial connection I might have shared with Hunter pales in comparison. I slip the letters I have back underneath the paper lining for safekeeping.

I want to *feel* what I must have felt for Thomas when he wrote these letters. No wonder he's been so odd since my overdose. How must it be to feel such burning passion for someone, to have shared such a love, only to have the other person forget you completely?

Suddenly, I remember Lyrica, the woman who Tabitha, the drained mystic from the coffee shop, told me about. Maybe if I sneak into the Depths and find her, she can help restore my memories to me. I have to at least *try*. I owe it to myself, and to Thomas. *Romeo.*

I change my clothes, throw on a pair of dark running shoes and a cap to cover my face, and, on a whim, stuff Davida's gloves into my back pocket. Maybe, if I can find her, Lyrica can explain what's so special about them.

A few pillows under my sheets and anyone who casually looks in will think it's me asleep in the dark.

I tiptoe to my door, pressing it open. Before I take another step, an image pops into my head: myself, in the Depths—

"You came," he says.

"Of course I did."

From his neck down I can see everything—the stiff collar of his shirt, the tanned skin of his forearms—but everything above that is shrouded in mystery, blurry and indistinct, as if he's a partly erased figure in a drawing.

I place my hand on his shoulder. "Look at me." He doesn't answer. "Please."

"Do you remember?" he asks softly.

I shake my head. "But maybe if I can just see you—"

He lifts his head to the light and I cry out: he has no face, only a sheet of white. His mouth is a thin red line. There are deep holes where his eyes should be.

"Remember," the ghost face says. "Remember me, Aria."

I snap out of the memory.

I'm trying, I think, clenching my fists. *I'm trying.*

· XI ·

The motorized gondola moves quickly through the rippling water, down the Broadway Canal. This, I notice, is one of the wider canals I've seen in the Depths—plenty of gondolas can travel back and forth without fear of collision, as well as a handful of the larger water taxis.

We turn down a waterway that is significantly narrower and darker. If there are street numbers etched onto the walls of these older buildings, I can't make them out on the broken brick and peeling paint. There are no light posts here, only mystic-lit sconces and those are far and few between. Most entryways at the water level are covered with locked gates that are crumbling and brown with age. Greenish-yellow algae clings to the bottom of these buildings, tangled like knotty hair after a shower, floating on the water in large clumps.

Eventually, my gondolier pulls up to a rickety wooden dock and lassos one of the posts. He gives the rope a yank and pulls us in. I pay him and in a moment am on the dock. Before I can even thank him, he has removed the rope and set off.

A few apartments give off hints of light above me, and I can see lines of laundry crossing the narrow canal, undershirts flapping in the hot breeze. In the spaces between the tall buildings, the brightness of the spires around the Magnificent Block pulses like a heartbeat in a language I don't understand.

I think of Tabitha—*follow the lights*—and wonder how I'm supposed to do that when I can't even find the address she gave me for Lyrica: 481 Columbus Avenue.

There are campaign posters on the brick walls. They are mixed with hateful graffiti: the words FOSTER and ROSE crossed out or covered with profanity. I lower my cap, determined not to be identified this time around.

Homeless people seem as much a part of the streets as the buildings—young children, grandparents, and every age in between—all with the same weathered faces, tired eyes, dirt-caked skin. They're not mystics, so why aren't we taking care of them?

"You lost, miss?" one woman asks me.

I nod. "Do you know where Columbus Avenue is? Four eighty-one?"

The woman points. I thank her and I head off.

I know I must be getting closer to the Block when I notice the election posters have changed. *These* posters haven't been vandalized. A woman with blond hair stares out at me, smiling. She looks about my mother's age, dressed in a navy-blue blazer and a crisp white blouse. Her face radiates intelligence and warmth. VOTE FOR CHANGE, the poster reads. VOTE FOR VIOLET.

So this is Violet Brooks. The mystic who's running against Garland. Something about her is familiar to me, though I have no idea why.

Finally, the narrow street opens out onto a major road where a series of bridges crosses the wide canal, leading into what must be the Magnificent Block. The canal circles the Block like a moat around a castle, flimsy-looking tenements peeking out from behind a massive stone wall.

Now I can see the numbers on the buildings. I pick up my pace, wiping the sweat from my forehead. Number 477. Bricks that might have once been red are brown with filth. Number 479 is a building with a ratty blue-and-white awning. And the next building should be 481—

Only, the number reads *483*. What's going on here?

I step up to the wooden door—it looks two or three knocks from falling apart—and peer through the window next to it. I can't see anything at first, so I wipe a tiny circle with my hand—dirt immediately greases my fingertips. The inside is completely empty, flooded ankle-deep with water. No one home here.

I go back to 479. The door is hidden behind an iron gate. On the gate is a buzzer with one bronze button. I push it. Maybe there *was* a 481 once upon a time, but it's certainly not around anymore. Did Tabitha give me the wrong address?

I feel utterly defeated. I've come all this way and risked so much in the hope that Lyrica can help me. And now it's as though she and her home don't even exist.

I pace in front of the buildings one last time and press my fingers to the space where 481 should be. The brick is rough beneath my hands. With my index finger, I draw an imaginary line and sigh.

And then the buildings begin to part.

There's no noise, really, only a gentle groan as the bricks start to separate smoothly, slowly, until another much shorter, warmer-looking building appears. No one, not even the homeless people nearby, is paying any attention. I wonder if they can even see what's happening.

The tiny building has orange stucco walls and two large windows that face the street. They're lit with red candles that flicker against the glass. A metal door swings open, and a woman who can only be Lyrica is standing inside.

She opens her mouth and I can see that she is missing a few teeth, her gums more black than pink. "You rang?" she asks.

The house smells wonderfully of cinnamon.

I follow Lyrica past a large wooden staircase, down a zigzagging hallway, into a sitting room on the left. Oriental tapestries adorn the walls, and yellow and green Chinese paper lanterns hang from the ceiling. What look like hieroglyphics are etched in charcoal onto the painted walls.

Lyrica, in her embroidered silk robe, motions for me to sit on a low sofa. "I have not met you before," she says, taking a seat opposite me. There is a strange beauty about her: her gray hair is in thin braids woven with colored beads and gold threads. Her skin is toffee-colored and mostly smooth; her only wrinkles are crow's-feet that spread from the corners of her eyes and a few laugh lines around her mouth.

I am still in shock from the magic I witnessed. "How did you—"

"This place is protected," Lyrica tells me. "From those who

have hunted me before. Not just anyone can seek my help." She stares deeply into my eyes. "Only those who are truly in need."

"I am truly in need."

She nods in agreement. "But of course! You're here! What is your name?"

"Beth," I say. I feel uncomfortable being dishonest, but I want her help—and I doubt that anyone who lives in the Depths wants to help the daughter of Johnny Rose. I take off my cap and place it beside me.

"Beth," Lyrica says slowly, as though she has never heard the name before. "Why have you sought my aid?"

"My memories," I say. "I seem to have . . . lost them."

Lyrica raises her thick eyebrows. "How does one lose one's memories, child?"

I tell Lyrica about my overdose, waking up with no memory of my affair with Thomas. About my trip to the doctor and the strange sensations that followed, feeling suddenly in love with Thomas, then out of love just as easily. I tell her about the dream I've been having, the boy whose face I cannot see. About the love letters. "I just want to remember that I love him before we marry," I find myself saying. "And I have nowhere else to go."

Lyrica, whose eyes have been trained on me the entire time I've been speaking, glances at a glass orb that hangs from the ceiling. After a moment, her eyes seem to brighten—and the orb suddenly swirls with light.

"May I touch you?" She scoots closer, so that we are only inches from each other. "That is how I work best."

"Yes, if it will help."

She stretches out her fingers and leans forward. As soon as she touches my temples, a jolt of energy passes through my body. It shoots down my legs and up my arms, kicking me backward.

"Whoa!" I jump from the sofa. Lyrica looks startled and gathers her hands in her lap. "You haven't been drained."

Lyrica looks at me as though my statement is the most obvious thing in the world. "And?"

I sit back down, pressing my knees together. *The touch of a mystic has the potential to kill a human,* I remind myself. "Be gentle. Please."

Lyrica instructs me to close my eyes. Again she presses her hands to my temples; I feel the same initial jolt; then it fades to a dull warmth that flows through my limbs.

As her energy washes through me, flashes of memory fracture and spin in my mind: images of friends and family, of Thomas, of my parents, of Hunter and Turk and the drained mystics in the Depths, and of my dream of the mysterious boy.

"Open," Lyrica commands, and I raise my eyelids.

Her hands are out in front of her—a green glow emanates from each of her fingertips. It reminds me of Hunter, when he fought off the boys who were trying to hurt me, when he healed my wound with his touch. The light seems solid enough to reach out and touch, only I'm afraid of what might happen if I do.

Just when I grow used to seeing this strange vision before me, Lyrica snaps her fingers. The glow disappears, and a calm washes over her face.

"Would you like a cup of tea?" she asks suddenly.

"Um, sure," I say.

She walks to the back of the room, through a doorway covered by champagne-colored curtains that drape down from the ceiling, and returns with two ceramic mugs. She hands me one—bits of tea leaves and tiny twigs are clumped together at the bottom of the mug, swirling in the water.

"Here," she says, dipping her finger into my tea. I watch as the water begins to heat and bubble. Then she does the same for her mug. "Don't worry," she says. "I washed my hands."

"You can heat water with your finger?" I ask. Not that I'm surprised, really—it's clear that she can perform magic.

Lyrica chuckles. "You are thinking this is not so useful, eh? This same finger, child, can burn a hole right through your skin, into your skull, and singe your brain within a matter of seconds." She takes in my shocked expression. "I can also grill a panini by pressing it between my hands. You'd be surprised how useful that is." She sips her tea and I sip mine. It tastes good, like oranges and mint.

"So," I say. "Did you see anything, erm, interesting? In my head?"

Lyrica sets down her mug. "I will be direct with you. That is the best way." She inhales dramatically, and a few of the candles in the hallway flicker. "Someone has tampered with your memories. But whoever did it has performed an incomplete job."

Tampered with my memories? "What do you mean?" I ask.

"You went to the doctor and had an operation. Is that correct?"

"Not an operation, exactly." I think back to my visit with Dr. May. "But I went through a machine and was given a series of shots. I did remember a little bit afterward, but the memories I had were . . . strange."

I think of that dinner out with Thomas, the strange voice inside my head, the intense feeling of being in love with him, wanting him. Then I think of how that feeling vanished. I think of being in Thomas's bedroom, of the story he told me about us being together in the gondola. Of how I began to see a picture in my mind—but his image was distorted. The colors were all wrong, and nothing felt natural.

"But that happened recently," I say. "I'm still missing memories as a result of my overdose. I don't understand the connection between the two."

"Maybe you only *think* you've been to the doctor once, or had one operation," Lyrica says, pursing her cracked lips. "Down here we call that tampering magic. Tell me more about this overdose."

"I don't remember," I admit. "I OD'd on Stic. I've been told that I nearly died, but that the doctors managed to save me—"

She cuts me off with a vigorous head shake.

"You have never ingested Stic," she says. "I can tell that from the way your body works. Everything inside you speaks, you see, and I just spoke to your body. I read your organs and your blood, and there is no trace of mystic energy there."

"Are you sure? I was told—"

"Whoever has told you this is deceiving you," Lyrica says. "I suppose you had at least two procedures—the first to wipe away the old memories, and a second to put in the new ones."

My breath feels caught in my throat. I *didn't* overdose on Stic. A medical procedure was responsible for removing my memories.

Thomas. This explains why I can't remember anything about our relationship.

"The elimination of these targeted memories was successful, but the planting of the new memories—that was not. That is why the second procedure was performed," Lyrica says. "Only, seeing you now, I do not believe that worked properly, either."

What was it my mother said to Dr. May? *The last time was such a failure.*

Why would anyone want to remove memories simply to implant the same ones a few weeks later? And why would my parents lie to me about my overdosing?

"Is it possible for me to regain those memories? The ones that were removed?"

Lyrica purses her lips sadly. "Not unless they were saved when they were removed. There are ways to contain memories, to fold them up and tuck them away in case they are needed in the future. But that is not medicine—it is magic. And complicated magic, at that." She picks up her tea and takes another sip. I glance down and realize that I've finished mine. "But it is possible. If you were to find the container for those memories, you might be able to release them. But even that is a delicate procedure. And quite a dangerous one."

My heart sinks. I was hoping there would be some easy way, some quick fix.

"But here is the question I have," Lyrica says, her dark irises glittering with something otherworldly. "What kind of memories did you have that were so important someone would want to risk your life to make them go away? And who would do this to you?"

A silence seems to strangle the room. I know the answer to her question, but I don't want to speak it aloud: *My family is risking my life to make me forget.*

I hold out my empty mug. How long have I been here? Minutes or hours? I have no idea.

"Thank you for your help." I dig into my pockets for something to pay her with, and set the gloves beside me on the couch. "I don't know what you charge, but—"

"Where did you get those?" Lyrica snaps. Before I can stop her, she reaches over and grabs Davida's gloves. "You're using these to travel the rail undetected? Is that how you got here, child? Who gave these to you?"

"I have no idea what you mean," I say, snatching them back from her.

"These gloves," Lyrica says, "are enchanted."

Why would Davida have enchanted gloves—and where did she get them?

"See the fingertips?" Lyrica points to the curious whorls I noticed when I first saw the gloves. "The tips are layered with fingerprints, thousands of them—fictional people, people who have died years ago, whoever. Their prints are there, stitched into the very fabric, and they cannot be scratched away. Anyone who wears these gloves can use the rail or the PODs and go unrecognized by the scanners. You'll register as someone other than yourself, and your identity changes every time you use them.

"Be careful with those, child." She turns her head. "It is time for you to go."

At her front door, she touches my shoulder. "Goodbye, Aria, and good luck."

I leave 481 and don't look back. It's only once I'm gone that I realize Lyrica knew me all along.

· XII ·

I should be getting home.

There's so much to process. Thomas, my parents, Dr. May. But I'm distracted: sounds are coming from up ahead, inside the Block. I lift my cap and strain to see over the brick wall that encloses the area—sparks of colored light are shooting into the air like fireworks. What's going on?

Fragments of blue and red and pink light cut through the misty clouds, crisscrossing in a dazzling display. The colors make the area seem more welcoming; I feel drawn to it. The roar of a crowd fills my ears, a mixture of laughter and yelling and applause. Something incredibly festive is going on.

But what?

I wipe the moisture from my palms onto my pants. A few quick, purposeful strides and I'm on one of the bridges. The wall around the Block is massive and imposing, but there's a man-made break I pass through, and just like that, I am inside. No scans, no fingertouch. I guess people down here aren't so concerned with folks trying to break into the Block when so many are dying to get out.

Unlike the rest of the Depths, where at least some of the city pavement is walkable, the inside of the Block is mostly water. In order to cross it and still allow gondola access, mazelike steel walkways have been erected. The railings are slick and grimy, but I hold on to them anyway, scared I might topple over.

The walkway is wide enough for three or four people. I move slowly away from the Block entrance, toward . . . I don't know. There are other walkways parallel to the one I'm crossing; they seem to lead to the very center of the Block, though I have no idea what's *at* the center. From what I can tell, though, that's where the celebration is occurring, where the light is coming from.

I gaze up into the windows of the tenements as I walk past, but they seem to be deserted. The buildings in the Block are constructed on stilts, high enough to clear the water, and they continue far into the distance. A few people shuffle by me, paying me no heed. Then someone grips my upper arm and a surge of energy passes through me, like I'm being electrocuted.

"Whoa," I say, leaping backward and wrenching myself free. I turn to run but the hand grabs me again. *Oh God. I'm about to die.*

The figure wears a hood that covers his or her face. All I can see is sparks in the eyes as the figure leans close to me and says, "You shouldn't be out here." Then he shakes back his hood and I see that it's Hunter.

I sigh with relief. He looks even better than I remember. His sun-streaked hair is messy and he brushes it back with his hands. Under his cloak are a tight navy V-neck and a torn pair of jeans. His blue eyes glisten in the darkness.

"Why do you care where I go?" The question comes out more harshly than I intend.

"I don't. Not really." He bites his bottom lip and looks away. I can tell he's lying. Instead of making me mad, however, it sort of . . . flatters me. I remember Turk telling me how cryptic Hunter is, how difficult he can be to understand.

I glance ahead, into the Block. "Where are you going?"

He raises an eyebrow. "Where are *you* going?"

"Home."

"Through the Block?" I can tell he doesn't think this is a good idea. "Let me help. You look like you could use a tour guide."

"I can make it on my own."

Hunter shakes his head. "I'm not taking any chances with you. Come on, let's go." He pulls his hood back up, takes my hand—I feel a delicious tingle—and we're off.

At first, I'm surprised by Hunter's stealth—how he moves like a cat, how with his hood covering his face and his hands in his pockets, he practically blends into the night—but he *is* a rebel, after all. Used to hiding, disappearing. No wonder he hasn't been caught and imprisoned.

We're mostly silent as we move farther into the Block. I look up; on either side are ramshackle mystic homes with roofs that look like they might cave in at any second. The green-black water below gives off a salty, overwhelming smell. I can tell we're on a slight incline. We must have trekked a mile by now, though I don't know where we're heading.

The shouts up ahead seem to be getting louder. "Come on," Hunter says, glancing over his shoulder. "Slowpoke."

"I'm not slow!"

"You're like a snail. If we were in France, they'd cook you up."

"Oh, please."

Just when I least expect it, the walkway ends. Suddenly, my feet are on something soft—a mass of land has risen out of the water. I'm guessing we're at one of the highest points in the Block. "What's this?"

Hunter looks down. "Grass."

Oh! I've read about this in school—we don't have it in the Aeries. I stop and reach down, running my hands over the flecks of green and brown.

"Aria."

I jerk my attention back to Hunter. "Yes?"

"If you like the grass, you'll *love* the trees."

I flick my eyes up—as far as I can see there is land, more land than I have ever seen, sprinkled with real, live trees. Trees! They are thin and sickly and nothing like the plush plants in the Aeries greenhouses, but here they are. I'm surprised that no one in the Aeries seems to know this all exists.

"You know, it wasn't always like this," Hunter says. Walking next to him makes me feel protected. I can't help but notice the muscles in his arms, bulging against the cotton sleeves of his shirt.

"Like what?" I ask.

"So run-down and tired. The Block used to be beautiful—the hub of the city."

I look around and scrunch up my nose. "What happened?"

"You've heard of Ezra Brooks, obviously," Hunter says.

"Who?"

Hunter's jaw goes slack. "Well, you know about the Conflagration, don't you?"

I think back to what I learned at Florence Academy. "Of course. It was an attack on the city. Now it is a day of mourning, when we remember the hundreds of lives that were lost because of the mystic bomb."

"Ezra Brooks died in the Conflagration. He was the representative the mystics had chosen to run in the election against your family and the Fosters' man. Ezra tried to convince the city to pay for renovations to restore the Block to its former glory. When he died, the government abandoned that plan and made it the only place mystics were legally allowed to live—the most undesirable part of all Manhattan."

"Undesirable? But there's solid ground here," I say. "There's nothing like this in the Aeries."

"True. But think how much hotter it is down here than all the way up there. Nobody who doesn't have to would want to live in the Depths. Besides, there isn't *that* much land."

I look around. It seems sad that all this is hidden, but I suppose it does make sense. "And this Ezra Brooks . . . he was a mystic?"

"Yes. He was a great man, actually," Hunter tells me as we walk past a grouping of shacks, their windows open and bare, their roofs missing shingles and patches of paint.

I think of the campaign posters I saw on the way to Lyrica's house. "Was he related to Violet Brooks?"

"Sure was," Hunter says. "She's his daughter."

I stop. There's a window up ahead with light streaming out; I can see a family—a young man and woman and a child—sitting at a table, eating dinner.

"Nonmystics weren't the only people who died during the explosion, you know," Hunter says. "We lost a lot of people ourselves—innocents who did nothing wrong.

"After the Conflagration the city started the mystic drainings and forced us all to live in the Block." Hunter stops, seeing me staring at the family. "That's the Terradills, Elly and Nic. They have a baby around five months old. Nic owns a gondola with a few other men, and that's how he makes a living."

"Are you friends with them?" I ask.

Hunter considers this. "Friends? Not really. But everyone in the Block knows everyone else. It's a pretty tight-knit community."

As we walk, Hunter points out the homes of other mystic families, most of whom either own gondolas and make their money independently or work in the Depths for the government, operating water taxis, disposing of garbage, performing building maintenance, and doing other mundane jobs. The way he talks about them makes it seem like he knows them all intimately.

"The farther in the house is—closer to the Great Lawn—the more money a family has." He eyes my clutch and my shoes. "Of course, that's relative. It's not even close to, you know, how much money people have in the Aeries."

I try to smile—Hunter is skirting the issue that my family is one of the reasons why all these people suffer, why they all live in such horrid conditions without enough money or food. I suddenly feel sick to my stomach.

"And where do you live?" I ask to change the subject. "Up ahead, where the noise is?" The sounds—music, and commotion, and children screaming playfully—have grown louder as we've worked our way deeper into the Block.

Hunter doesn't answer. "Come on," he says. "There's a POD only a few hundred yards that way, just outside the Block."

"Wait," I say at the same time that he goes to grab my hand. Our fingers touch and my hand buzzes with energy.

He pulls away. "Sorry. I forget how dangerous my touch can be to you—I'm not used to dealing with . . ."

"Nonmystics?"

Hunter cracks a grin. "I was going to say girls. But yeah, sure. Nonmystics."

I feel myself blush—thank God it's dark and he can't see. "Well, don't be sorry. Be careful." For the first time in a long while, I feel relaxed, despite being in this strange, dangerous part of the city. It might have something to do with what Lyrica told me, but I also know it has a lot to do with Hunter, with how he puts me at ease. "I'm not ready to go home just yet."

Hunter's face brightens. "Really?"

Just then, we hear what sounds like a miniature rocket blast in the sky. "Where is all that noise coming from?"

"The carnival," Hunter says. "It doesn't happen often, but it's a great time. Everybody lets their hair down and forgets their worries. For a night, anyway."

"What's a carnival?"

Hunter looks shocked. "Seriously? Well, come on. We can't let you leave the Block without having a bit of fun."

The carnival is the liveliest thing I've ever seen. It's sort of like a plummet party, only instead of celebrating destruction, everyone here seems to be celebrating *life*.

Hunter leads me through a labyrinth of booths with mystics inside them selling their wares—tiny trinkets and dolls and wooden shoes, rows of buns and muffins and candies and chocolates, dresses made of thin material that waves in the wind, and hats, gloves, belts, and more.

Mystics pass me with plates of fried dough, their hands covered in powdered sugar. "Look!" I point to a tank full of water, where a young mystic is sitting, waiting to be dunked. He's soaking wet, which makes me think he's already been submerged. A few feet away, a group of kids are lined up, throwing tiny balls at the lever on the tank and hoping they'll sink him again.

"Looks cold," Hunter says, rubbing his arms. "Want one?" He motions to a booth full of stuffed animals, the kind my mother would never allow me to have when I was younger: teddy bears with bows around their necks, plush giraffes and monkeys and other exotic animals you'd find in a zoo.

"Sure," I say. "Only I don't have any credit here, and I'm almost out of coins—"

Hunter scoffs. "Aria, you can't just *buy* one of these."

"You can't?"

"Nope." He motions to the woman behind the booth, who nods and hands over five plastic rings, all in different colors. They look like cheap, oversized bracelets. Light from the carnival brightens his face. "You gotta win 'em."

She holds out her hand and helps me down. Turk wheels the motorcycle over to an old fire hydrant. He unwraps a chain from around the body of the bike, then locks the cycle to the hydrant.

When he's done, he searches for us in the dark—practically all I can make out are the whites of his eyes. "There's a spire somewhere around here," he says. "We should be able to get more light if we keep moving."

We walk together silently. I grab Turk's shirt and follow him. I hope he knows where he's going. My feet crunch over bits of broken pavement, an empty soda can. I can't see the Broadway Canal, but I know it's near us—I hear the slap of water hitting concrete and smell the foul, salty stench.

We go another block or two and turn right, over a bridge, and then I see a spire in the distance. Its light blankets the area with an iridescent glow. The familiar energy inside swirls and undulates white-yellow-green, white-yellow-green. I listen for signs of Hunter, of my parents, but all I hear are the muted voices of passersby in the distance, the shuffling of our feet, and the wild beating of my own nervous heart.

The neighborhood looks seedy. The streets are full of trash, the store windows covered with graffiti or smashed in. The buildings here seem crowded, overlapping like crooked teeth. Rats scurry along carrying bits of paper and rotting food. Overhead, faded marquees hang sadly from abandoned theaters, lightbulbs crushed or missing, windows smashed in.

"This used to be the center of the city," Turk says as we pass a wide intersection of avenues. A green sign that says 42ND STREET hangs from a post on one of the bridges. I see the entrance to the old subway station—the biggest I've encountered so far. Circles of different colors, red, yellow, blue, each with a faded number inside, are painted over the entrance.

I glance behind me to make sure Elissa is okay. She's peering around wildly, as if searching for someone. When our eyes meet, she looks guilty for a second; then she relaxes and gives me a tight grin.

"Is that how we get underground?" I point to the subway entrance, which is sealed with blocks of concrete laced with steel girders. It looks all but impenetrable. I search out the green posts, like the ones near the South Street Seaport, but I don't see any. I wonder how we'll get in.

Turk shakes his head. "No. The entrance is up there." He points a few blocks ahead: I don't see anything except a dirty, oversized sign about half the length of a city block. It was probably white at one point, but that was many years ago. Now it's a filthy beige, with large red block letters: TKTS.

"There?"

Turk nods. "Come on. But careful." He steps in front, motioning for us to follow; behind him, we stand pressed up against the wall of one of the buildings. There's a drooping awning overhead that's providing us with some well-needed shadow: the center of Times Square is bright, brighter than I anticipated. We'll have to stay around the edges so as not to be seen.

Turk listens carefully, then signals for us to proceed. I make sure I don't step on anything that might break and give us away. The closer we get to the TKTS sign, the more voices I hear. I look out toward the middle of the square.

And that's when I see him. A block away.

"Come on, boy," someone says. Hunter's head is down, his arms cuffed behind his back. His shoulders slump forward; he shuffles his feet as if it's painful to walk. There's a guard on either side of him, Stiggson and Klartino following directly behind. My father and George Foster walk a few feet ahead, bodyguards flanking them, along with Thomas, Garland, Kyle, and Benedict. None of the women are there.

I cover my mouth so they can't hear me gasp.

I poke Turk in the back and we stop in our tracks. Elissa, too. "What's happening?"

"Shhh," Turk hisses.

We press so close to the building that I can feel the bricks making imprints on my back and the palms of my hands. From this angle, we can see Hunter and my father's crew, but unless they come around the corner and run smack into us, we should remain out of sight.

We watch as the guards pull Hunter toward one of the buildings with a faded gold door. The windows are blackened with grime. "Is it this one?"

Hunter studies the door for a second. He's barely recognizable, his face is so bruised. His forehead is sliced open, his cheeks red and swollen. His hair is streaked with blood and matted to his head with sweat. My stomach feels like it's being wrung out. I might be sick.

"Don't recall," Hunter mutters.

My father strolls over to him, lifts his chin in the air with one finger. The sleeves of Dad's dress shirt are rolled up, exposing his thick forearms and the corded muscle there. Hunter tries to look away, but Dad grabs his jaw. "Look at me," he instructs.

For a second, they stare at each other—then Hunter spits at my father.

As soon as the spit hits his forehead, Dad attacks. He pulls back his arm and punches Hunter in the gut, then on the right side of the face. His fist connects with Hunter's chin with a loud smack.

Hunter doubles over, vomiting blood and bile and whatever else is in his stomach onto the pavement.

"Ready to stop the bullshit and show us where the entrance is?" my father asks.

Hunter doesn't answer. His lip is split—I can see that from here—and his eyes seem snuffed out, lifeless.

"I can't see," Elissa whispers from behind me. She shifts her weight forward and kicks something out from behind her—an empty glass bottle? I don't know, but it makes a sound that alerts everyone to our presence.

My entire body tenses, and I hold my breath. Turk's eyes are wide, alert. Nervous.

The guards raise their noses in the air like trained dogs, and I see my father whip his head around. Kyle, who's standing a few feet away with a pistol trained on Hunter, turns. "Who's there?" he shouts.

Elissa squeezes my hand, and I squeeze Turk's. I'm so scared. Maybe if we're quiet . . . *really* quiet . . . they'll ignore us.

Just then, someone stumbles over a bridge on the far side of the square. A man, from the looks of it, a bottle of booze in one hand. He turns onto the street where my father and the others are and freezes.

Kyle shoots.

The bullet lodges right in the man's forehead. The bottle falls, smashing on the ground, and the man drops to the pavement like an abandoned marionette.

"Just some drunk," Kyle calls out.

Relieved to have found the source of the noise, Dad and his goons shove Hunter to another derelict storefront. But for a split second I see Hunter glancing in our direction—there's a flash of life in his eyes.

He knows we're here.

I hope with all my heart that he'll lead my father away.

And then, as if he can hear my prayers, he opens his bloodied mouth and says, "Okay. I'll show you. It's down this alleyway."

He points in the opposite direction of the sign, and I know he's lying, trying to buy us more time. The goons hold their guns to his back, piloting him forward, their figures diminishing as they move into the distance.

Turk pulls us away from the street corner and into a huddle. Then, finally, he lets go of my hand. "While Hunter is distracting them, we need to go underground and get with reinforcements. We can outnumber them." Turk points to the ratty TKTS sign. "See the gray building just under the sign?" We nod. "That's where the entrance is. We'll rescue Hunter and disappear back into the subways, where we can figure out our next move."

"Sounds like a plan," I say, relieved to have one.

"I've never used that entrance," Elissa says, nodding toward the banded cement blocks. She doesn't apologize for making noise— for almost getting us killed. Shadows and light from Times Square play on her face, making her seem older than she is. "How will I get in?"

Turk rolls his eyes; I can tell he wishes she weren't here. He swipes a hand over his hair. The rain has flattened down his Mohawk, which sweeps over to one side. "Aria has a passkey." I raise my hand, wiggle my finger with the ring on it. It's the only part of my body that feels warm. Elissa's eyes shine with recognition.

"You'll have to grab her hand when she uses it," Turk instructs. "You both should be able to gain entrance that way. I'm going to stay here, make sure they don't hurt him too bad."

"But I don't know where anything is down there," I say. "I'm not sure I could even find Hunter's place by myself. What if I get lost? And besides, who will listen to me? You two go. I'll stay here and watch out for Hunter."

Turk shakes his head. "Absolutely not, Aria. I'm not leaving you up here alone." He sighs. "We'll all go together, then, and hope nothing happens to Hunter in the meantime."

"Then let's go," Elissa says confidently, standing up straight.

We wait for the perfect second to break. As soon as my father's group is out of sight, Turk waves his hand and whispers, "Now!"

We bolt out of the shadows, high-stepping over a pile of broken cobblestones and dashing along a wide, high bridge that crosses the canal. There before us is the entrance, just beneath the faded sign. Like the old subway entrances, this, too, is sealed with steel-reinforced concrete.

Then I notice a spindly post, practically hidden behind the wall of concrete. It's made of metal, and at the top is a small green globe. It must have been decorative at one point, but now it's fused to the steel, bent, so that if you weren't looking for it, you certainly wouldn't find it.

"The globe," I say. "It's a smaller version of the ones at the Seaport."

I'm reaching for it when I hear a gunshot.

I look over my shoulder and Turk is on the ground, grabbing his chest. A plume of blood has blossomed on his T-shirt and is seeping through his fingers. His face is frozen in shock.

"Elissa, watch out!" I say, but then I see the expression on her face: she's grinning, her smile wicked and dark.

And then I notice the gun in her hand.

She shot Turk.

Before I can react, Elissa grabs my hand and twists off the ring Turk gave me: the passkey.

"Elissa, what are you doing? I thought . . ."

"You thought wrong," she sneers, laughing triumphantly. "I work for your parents, and the Fosters, hunting out rebels. That's my real job. No one, not even Patrick, knows the truth." She takes a deep breath.

"How long have you been doing this?" I ask, trying to keep her talking, hoping to think of something, anything, that will allow me to escape.

"The Conflagration?" Elissa says. "The bomb was *my* pet project, made from *my* energy."

It all makes sense now: Elissa was the one who turned against her people for personal gain, who was given a spot in the Aeries and hired by my parents to get the mystics out of the picture. She must have been in her early twenties then, and she's been working for my family ever since.

Elissa runs back out into the street. "I have the passkey!" She holds the ring above her head like a trophy. "And I've found the entrance!"

There's a sinking feeling in my stomach. I've been betrayed. Turk's been shot. And now I am about to die.

· XXXI ·

Suddenly, Times Square is alive with movement.

Armored men creep out of buildings and onto the streets like ants, crawling over bridges, lining up to penetrate and attack. Some of the men I recognize as my father's supporters, or George Foster's; others must be part of the city's police force, which my father and George have in their back pockets.

There's no time to think. I just *do*.

I grab Turk by the armpits and drag him underneath the sign, which hangs diagonally and blocks us from view. My palms are sweaty, and he's heavier than I expected. His eyes are shut in pain.

I hear the sound of commands being hollered into the air, of dozens of feet approaching. It's stopped raining now, and the air is damp and hot. Any second, my father will be back with Hunter. There's only one thing I can do.

I let Turk down to the pavement, then grab the green globe. With my free hand, I reach across Turk's chest, pulling his arm so that his fingers touch the globe, too.

The ground beneath me liquefies.

My body begins to thrum as though drumbeats are reverberating through the ground, throbbing in my bones. There's a weird sensation like being squeezed through an ultrathin tube. I close my eyes.

We fall. . . .

And land on a dirty tiled floor. It used to be white, I think. Huge chunks are missing. Along the ceiling are colored circles like the ones outside the subway entrance. At one time, they must have pointed to specific trains.

Ahead of me is a network of tunnels that branch out in different directions. I seem to be on a platform of some sort: to my left are old stairways that lead down to tunnels full of water, lined with high catwalks like down at the Seaport. To my right is a wall covered in graffiti and old, unrecognizable ads. Ahead is darkness.

I look up and see that a few lights seem to be embedded in the walls. If they're anything like the ones down at the Seaport, they're likely motion sensitive. I need the light, but I don't want to leave Turk, and he's in no position to walk.

I kneel beside him and check his pulse—it's faint but there. Still, I know the wound will be fatal if he bleeds out before I can get him any help.

I bite the end of my sleeve and rip off a piece of my shirt, which I crumple into a ball and hold to Turk's wound, letting it sop up the blood. Overhead, the stomping of feet is heavy, as if there are a thousand men above us.

"Turk? Can you hear me?"

Nothing.

·ACKNOWLEDGMENTS·

Thank you:

To everyone at Random House Children's Books, especially Françoise Bui, for her fierce insight and support, Colleen Fellingham, Kenny Holcomb, and the incomparable Beverly Horowitz.

To my parents, Elizabeth and Steven Malawer, my family, and my friends, especially Blair Bodine—who encouraged this novel when it was just an idea on a train to Boston—Kate Berthold, Julia Alexander, Anna Posner, Nic Cory, and my sister, Abby, who has always been my biggest fan. Special thanks to Ruth Katcher, Paul Wright, Dan Kessler, and Bronwen Durocher for their early reads and thoughtful comments. To Stephanie Elliott for seeing a spark in the darkness, and to Christopher Stengel for his design ingenuity.

To Michael Stearns, for being a tireless thinker, a brilliant teacher, and a wonderful friend. Your sense of story and language brought *Mystic City* to life. This book simply would not exist without you.

And lastly to Josh Pultz, who is—above all—a true peach.

RENEGADE HEART

A MYSTIC CITY Novel, Book II

Summer 2013

Delacorte Press

About the Author

Theo Lawrence was born in 1984 and is a graduate of Columbia University and the Juilliard School. A Presidential Scholar in the Arts for Voice, he has performed at Carnegie Hall and the Kennedy Center as well as Off-Broadway. He is pursuing a master's degree in literature at Fordham University and lives on Manhattan's Upper West Side. His apartment is full of pictures of dachshunds.